ROCK TOONS

A CARTOON HISTORY OF THE FIRST 30 YEARS OF ROCK'N'ROLL

ARTWORK : SERGE DUTFOY
SCENARIO : MICHAEL SADLER
ROCKOLOGY : DOMINIQUE FARRAN
COLORS : SOPHIE BERNÈS
ENGLISH LANGUAGE VERSION : MICHAEL SADLER

HARMONY BOOKS
NEW YORK

Published by Harmony Books, a division of Crown Publishers, Inc.,
225 Park Avenue South, New York, New York 10003

Originally published in french as HISTOIRE DU ROCK en bandes dessinées,
by Editions Francis Van de Velde, 12, rue Jacob, 75006 Paris
Harmony and colophon are trademarks of Crown Publishers, Inc.
Manufactured in France
Library of Congress Cataloging-in-Publication Data TK

ISBN 0-517-56325-8
10 9 8 7 6 5 4 3 2 1

First American Edition

Imprimé en France par l'Imprimerie du Marval à Vitry
Dépôt légal n° 2131 - Avril 1986
46.10.0235.93

46.0235.5
86.4

LOOK THEY SAID... OOH LA LA...
VAN DER PLOOK PUBLISHER
... VERY TRICKY, VERY DICEY ... ALL THAT HISTORY, ALL THOSE DATES, ALL THOSE MOVEMENTS - SOCIO, POLITICO, MUSICO, COMPLEXO-MIGRAINO... YOU GET THE PICTURE... PHEW!
THEN - CLICK - THE LIGHT CAME ON!
BRIGHT IDEA! HAND THE PROJECT OVER TO TEAM OF SPECIALISTS (ALL OF THEM REAL CATS..) ONLY THEY CAN TELL YOU ... ... THE HISTORY OF ROCK! ...
ALLOW ME TO INTRODUCE ... ...

THE EDITORIAL TEAM OF

CAT: THE EDITOR ... ... CUT OPEN HIS HEART, YOU'LL FIND THE WORD ROCK. FAVORITE RECORD: CHUCK BERRY: "ROCK AND ROLL MUSIC"

COOKIE: CAT'S ASSISTANT - A HOT NUMBER WITH THAT FELINE FEELING... FAVORITE RECORD: ELVIS PRESLEY: "LOVE ME TENDER"...

ANDRE: RESIDENT EGGHEAD: AUTHOR OF "HEAVY METAL AND METONYMY" (1977 - OUT OF PRINT.) FAVORITE GROUP: TALKING HEADS.

RAYMOND: (AND HIS DIRTY RAINCOAT) GUTTER PRESS SCANDAL MONGER AND PROUD OF IT ... FAVORITE RECORD: IAN DURY "SEX AND DRUGS AND ROCK 'N' ROLL".

MR BIRD: PRESENTER OF THE CARTOON HISTORY OF MUSIC A HIGHBROW AT SEA AMONG THE CAT ROCKERS. FAVORITE COMPOSER: SCRIABIN (POSEUR!)

JUST LISTEN TO HIM!
PUNK!!
RINGO STARR!
HUH!
... ROCK BEGINS WITH ... ...
HEAVY METAL!!?
CALL THAT ROCK?!
LOOK ... THE ONLY PLACE TO START IS ...
NO!
IT'S VAN DER PLOOK! HE WANTS CHAPTER ONE ...
PAUL ANKA (NUDGE NUDGE)
THE WORLD'S FIRST ROCKER? I'LL TELL YOU ...
WHEN??
...TONIGHT!
ELVIIIIIS
HIM??? YOU'RE JOKING...
LET'S TRY AND BE CONSTRUCTIVE!...
YOU MAD?!
CAT ROCK NEWS

THE BEGINNINGS OF ROCK

1954 ... THE COLD WAR (BRRR ...) SUDDENLY A U.F.O. APPEARS IN THE SKY ...
ZOOMS LIKE A METEOR THROUGH THE PAGES OF "VARIETY" ... ...
R
O
C
K
DORIS DAY
BING CROSBY
FRANK SINATRA
DEAN MARTIN
...AND LANDS-CRASH!!-ON UNSUSPECTING SHOWBIZ! IT'S ... NONE OTHER THAN ...
SHAKE RATTLE N' ROLL!
Gibson
BILL HALEY & HIS COMETS
WHERE DOES THIS NEW SOUND COME FROM? FROM C&W AND R&B!!
EXPLANATION PAGE 18.
WHO?

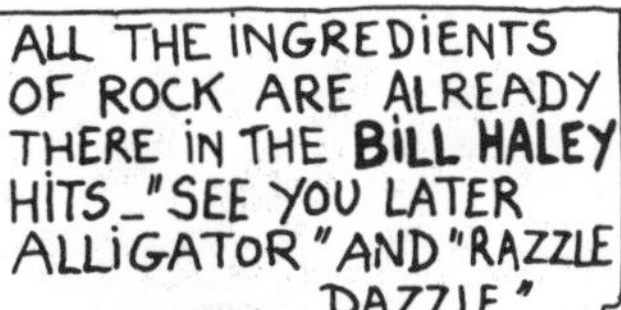
ALL THE INGREDIENTS OF ROCK ARE ALREADY THERE IN THE BILL HALEY HITS – "SEE YOU LATER ALLIGATOR" AND "RAZZLE DAZZLE"...

PULSATING RHYTHM ...

VOLUME ... ...

AMPLIFIED GUITAR ...

... VIBRATO ...

SHAKE!
...SIMPLE LYRICS ...

SHAKE!!
SHAKE!
REPEATED AGAIN AND AGAIN

SHAKE
...SCREAMED OUT ...

... ENERGY ...

...AGGRESSION ...

... STYLE ...

" THIS MUSIC IS GOING TO CHANGE THE WORLD ... ..."
BEFORE
SCHOOL
HOW ORDERLY AND DISCIPLINED! SUCH WONDERFUL BEHAVIOUR
"ROCK AROUND THE CLOCK", HALEY'S MUSIC FOR THE FILM "BLACKBOARD JUNGLE" BECOMES SYNONYMOUS WITH REVOLT !! ...
FLOP

AFTER
DZiiiNG.
THIS IS IT, CATS ! THE MUSIC OF OUR GENERATION !...
ROCK AROUND THE CLOCK
CLAP
SNAP
DAILY NEWS
NEW YORK
"ROCK 'N' ROLL LEADS STRAIGHT TO JUVENILE DELINQUENCY..."

ROCK SPRINGS FROM VARIOUS SOURCES...
FIRST FROM...
NEW ORLEANS
NEW ORLEANS
ROCKABILLY
CHICAGO ROCK
VOCAL GROUPS
TWO GREAT NAMES...
FATS DOMINO
BAD START TO FATS' CAREER. HIS HAND IS CRUSHED IN MACHINERY AT THE MATTRESS FACTORY WHERE HE WORKS!
DOO PAP A DOO DOO
WAOOOH!
PINK DREAMS
FATS SINGS AND PLAYS BOOGIE/WOOGIE WHOSE BASS LINE IS ONE OF THE CORNER-STONES OF ROCK...
1950: FATS' FIRST RECORD "THE FAT MAN"...
HE WEIGHS 275 POUNDS AND IS 5 FT. 3 IN. TALL
FATS FACTS
THE GREEN... ?!?
SCRATCH
A GOOD BUSINESSMAN, FATS IS FAST TO MAKE A FORTUNE...
SCRATCH
?!?
... OR THE PINK...
OWNING OVER A HUNDRED SUITS, TWO DOZEN CARS...
FATS' ROCK - AS THE TITLES OF HIS HITS INDICATE - IS HOMELY AND INNOCUOUS:
"BE MY GUEST"
"I'M READY"
"AIN'T THAT A SHAME!"
AND THE LEGENDARY "BLUEBERRY HILL", SUNG WITH HIS INIMITABLE NASAL VOICE AND CREOLE ACCENT.

ROCK
...AN EXOTIC MIXTURE OF MUSIC FROM SPAIN, FRANCE AND AFRICA...
BRASS AND SAX TO THE FORE, THE PIANO STEALING THE LIMELIGHT FROM THE GUITAR...
AFTER MR BIG, MR SMALL
AFTER MR PLACID, MR WILD!
LITTLE RICHARD
TWO PREACHER GRANDFATHERS, A WHISKY BOOTLEGGER FOR A FATHER...
RICHARD PENNIMAN WAS BORN IN 1932...
AWOP BOP ALOO BOP ALOP
HIS BACKGROUND EXPLAINS (?)...
THE FERVOUR AND THE SAVAGERY OF HIS VOLCANIC ROCK. "TUTTI FRUTTI" (1955) "LONG TALL SALLY" (1956) "LUCILLE" (1957) "GOOD GOLLY MISS MOLLY" (1958)...
BAM BOOM AWOP
THE ... UM ... LYRICS OF HIS ... ER ... SONGS ARE ARTICULATE EXPRESSIONS OF THE EMOTIONAL IMPULSE AT THE HEART OF THIS ... UM ... MUSIC?
awop bop aloo bop alop bam boom
To Cookie Little Richard
ON STAGE HE PREACHES THE OUTRAGEOUS ... ...
ALOO BOP ALOP BAM BOOM
WOW! THAT HAIR !!
IS IT REAL ??
AND LIPSTICK!
AND RINGS!
HE'S JUST GREAT!!
IF ONLY HE LOOKED LIKE ELVIS...
LITTLE RICHARD REMAINS DEEPLY INFLUENCED BY THE CHURCH ...
...WHEN FIRE BREAKS OUT ON THE PLANE TAKING HIM TO AUSTRALIA ... ...
...HE SWEARS TO ROCK NO MORE AND, TO ATONE, THROWS HIS JEWELS INTO SYDNEY HARBOUR ... ...
AWOP BOP ALOO BOP ALOP BAM
DING AWOP BOP DANG
GULP!...
YOU'RE RIGHT COBBER!

AFTER EXOTIC ROCK, RUSTIC ROCK, THE SOUND FROM THE STICKS ... ...
IN 1956, CARL PERKINS WRITES A SONG ABOUT HILLBILLIES, PROUD OF THEIR FLASH SUNDAY FOOTWEAR. "BLUE SUEDE SHOES" BECOMES THE ANTHEM OF A WHOLE GENERATION ...
?!
?!?
?
BL..
?
..UE SUEDE SHOES
ELVIIIIS
PERKINS BEGINS TO MAKE THE BIG TIME BUT...
... A CERTAIN ELVIS PRESLEY IS GOING TO STEAL HIS THUNDER ... AND HIS HIT! ...

... AN UNSOPHISTICATED ROCK FROM THE HICK-TOWNS AND BACKWOODS ...
= MIXTURE OF ROCK AND HILLBILLY...
MEMPHIS
SUN RECORDS
SAM PHILIPS
ICE CR

... THE ROCKABILLY OF JERRY LEE LEWIS IS MORE ELECTRIC ... HE SOUNDS LIKE HANK WILLIAMS BUT ON STAGE IS MORE LIKE A MANIC LITTLE RICHARD!
CRAZY ARMS
HIS TITLES EXPRESS HIS PENCHANT FOR PHYSICAL VIOLENCE... "WHOLE LOTTA SHAKIN' GOIN' ON"
AND "GREAT BALLS OF FIRE"... (1957)
HOW DISTURBINGLY FREUDIAN!
12

O TEMPORA O MORES
BIG SCANDAL IN 1958! HE MARRIES HIS COUSIN ... HIS RECORDS ARE BANNED ON THE AIR ...
... BUT HE LATER MAKES A COME-BACK, CASHING IN ON HIS DRACULA/BLUEBEARD IMAGE, CALLING HIMSELF
THE KILLER!

IN A MORE GENTLE MOOD, THE ROCKABILLY HARMONIES OF THE EVERLY BROTHERS, TINGED WITH NOSTALGIA FOR THE WOOD FIRES OF THE OLD LOG CABINS OF HOME ... THE VERY HEART OF COUNTRY AND WESTERN ...
BYE BYE LOVE (1957)
DON OR PHIL?
HOME SWEET HOME
BUT THEIR SOUND WILL TRAVEL, INFLUENCING THE BEATLES, THE BEACH BOYS, THE MAMAS & THE PAPAS, CROSBY STILLS AND NASH! ...

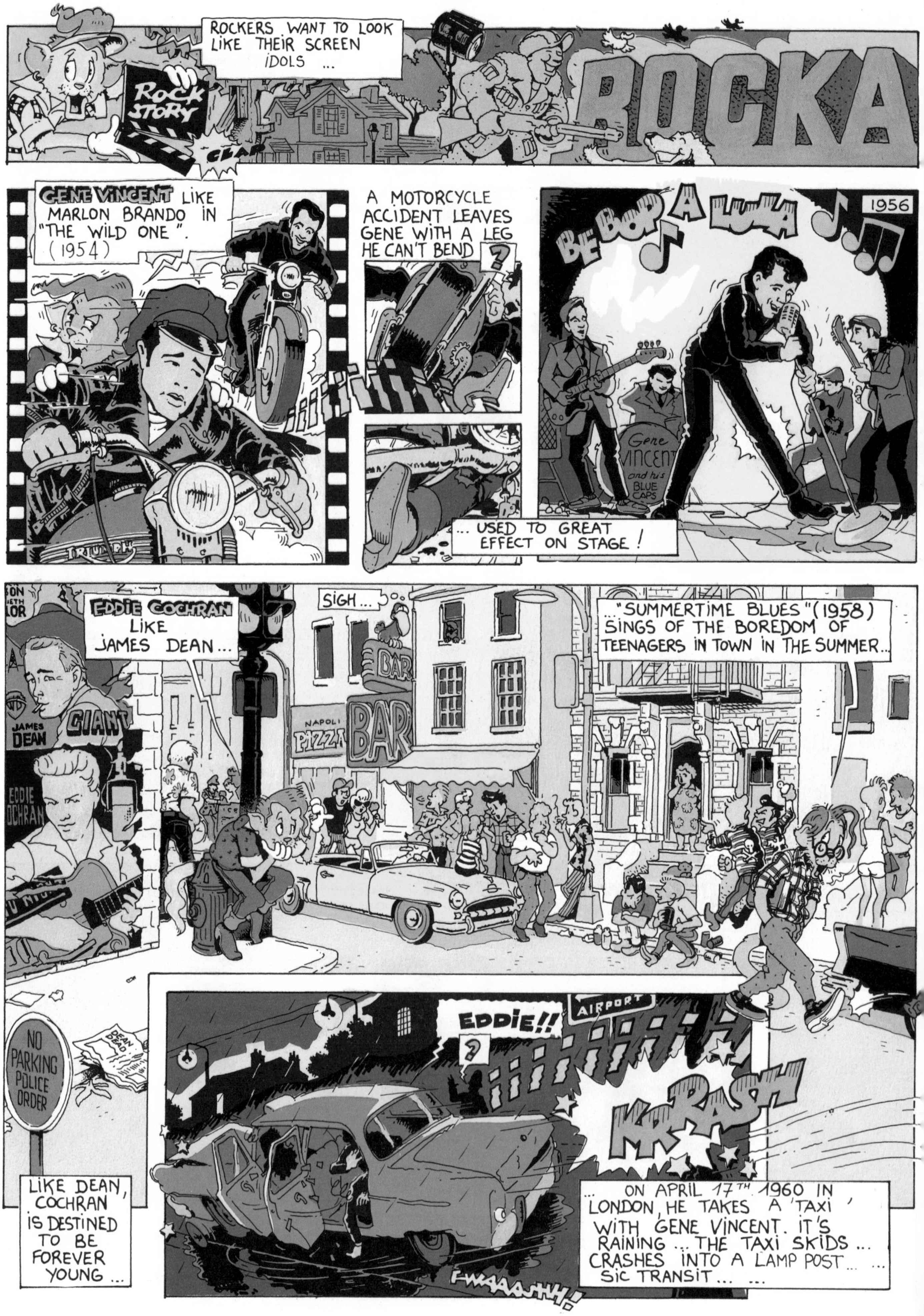

GENE VINCENT LIKE MARLON BRANDO IN "THE WILD ONE". (1954)

TRIUMPH

A MOTORCYCLE ACCIDENT LEAVES GENE WITH A LEG HE CAN'T BEND

?

BE BOP A LULA

1956

Gene VINCENT and his BLUE CAPS

... USED TO GREAT EFFECT ON STAGE!

EDDIE COCHRAN LIKE JAMES DEAN...

JAMES DEAN

GIANT

EDDIE COCHRAN

SIGH...

NAPOLI PIZZA

BAR

BAR

..."SUMMERTIME BLUES" (1958) SINGS OF THE BOREDOM OF TEENAGERS IN TOWN IN THE SUMMER...

NO PARKING POLICE ORDER

DEAN DEAD

EDDIE!!

?

AIRPORT

KRRASH

LIKE DEAN, COCHRAN IS DESTINED TO BE FOREVER YOUNG...

... ON APRIL 17TH 1960 IN LONDON, HE TAKES A 'TAXI' WITH GENE VINCENT. IT'S RAINING ... THE TAXI SKIDS ... CRASHES INTO A LAMP POST... ... SIC TRANSIT... ...

FWAAASHH!

BILLY
OR LIKE COMIC BOOK SUPERHEROES
COMICS
!
SUPERMAN
THE PUNY CHARLES HARDIN HOLLEY, BORN IN TEXAS IN 1936, IS INSPIRED BY COMICS... ...
...HE SEES HIMSELF AS CLARK KENT, THE SHY REPORTER, WHOSE SECRET IDENTITY IS SUPERMAN.
...ROCK WILL SOON TRANSFORM CHARLIE INTO BUDDY HOLLY-SUPERSTAR!... ...
IN NO TIME, THE JUKE-BOXES ARE FULL OF BUDDY HOLLY'S 45s
AMI
Multi Horn High fidelity
120 Selections
DAD'S
That'll be the day 1957. BUDDY HOLLY
Peggy Sue 1958. BUDDY HOLLY
May be baby 1958. BUDDY HOLLY
Think it over 1958 BUDDY HOLLY
BUDDY IS ONE OF THE FEW ROCKERS TO WEAR GLASSES ON STAGE!
...ELVIS COSTELLO TAKES A NOTE
* ALTHOUGH THE BIG 78s (PHEW!) STILL EXIST ... ...
THAT'LL BE THE DAY..
ALREADY ROCK STARS MAKE CRAZY TOURS - EVERY NIGHT A DIFFERENT TOWN...
..THAT I DIE!
...AND SO IT IS THAT ON FEBRUARY 1959, AT 1.30 A.M, BUDDY HOLLY'S PLANE CRASHES IN CLEAR LAKE, IOWA ... BUDDY WAS 23
WITH HOLLY AND COCHRAN, ROCK RUBS SHOULDERS WITH TRAGEDY...

NOTHING RUSTIC ABOUT...
CHICAGO

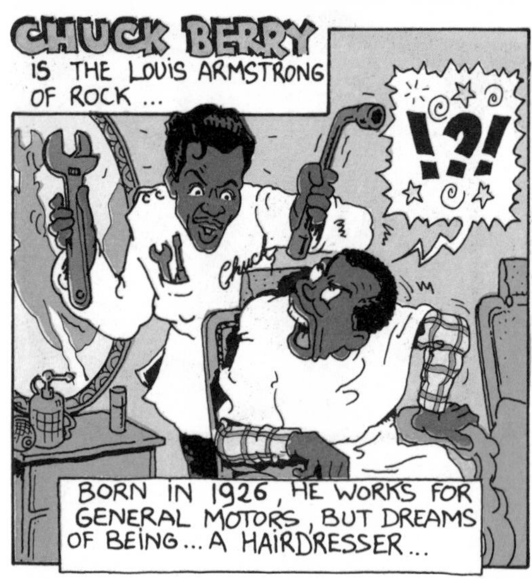
CHUCK BERRY IS THE LOUIS ARMSTRONG OF ROCK ...
!?!
BORN IN 1926, HE WORKS FOR GENERAL MOTORS, BUT DREAMS OF BEING... A HAIRDRESSER...

IN "JOHNNY B. GOODE" BERRY SINGS HIS OWN STORY - THE PRIMROSE PATH FROM RAGS TO RICHES...
RICHES
THE WOULD-BE BARBER IS THE FIRST REAL GUITAR HERO!

BERRY'S HITS SYSTEMATICALLY TREAT TEEN PROBLEMS - SCHOOL (TOUGH)... PARENTS (DIFFICULT)... CASH (HARD)... GIRLS (TRICKY)... ... ...
BARBER SHOP
IN "MAYBELLENE" (1955) A HOT RODDER PURSUES A HOT NUMBER IN A CADILLAC...
... AND ROCK EVEN SINGS OF... ROCK! IN "SCHOOL DAYS" AND "ROLL OVER BEETHOVEN" (1957)...
THANK GOD HE'S DEAF!
BEETHOVEN

DURING THIS PERIOD, WHICH SEES THE BEGINNING OF THE CIVIL RIGHTS MOVEMENT.

EQUAL RIGHTS
... BLACK MUSIC IS ONLY FOR BLACKS...

... THE BIG RECORD COMPANIES MAKE COVERS...

...A WHITE ARTIST SINGS A SYRUPY VERSION OF AN ORIGINAL BLACK NUMBER

SNAP
...PAT BOONE FOR EXAMPLE SINGS LITTLE RICHARD...

... BERRY IS LUCKY.. HIS CLEAR VOICE SOUNDS WHITE ON THE RADIO...

ROCK
MUDDY WATERS
...THE ROCK OF THE BLACKS IN THE CITIES, ROOTED IN R & B.
R & B?
WAIT FOR PAGE 18! ...

ON STAGE, CHUCK DEVISES THE DUCKWALK - HIS TRADEMARK! ... ...

BUT THERE ARE PROBLEMS IN THE WINGS ...
DUCKWALK THIS WAY, MY FRIEND.
AND IT'S IN PRISON THAT HE WRITES "SWEET LITTLE SIXTEEN"

...ON HIS RELEASE IN THE MID '60s THE NEW STARS OF THE ROCK SCENE ARE STILL SINGING HIS HITS ...
?
ROLL OVER BEETHOVEN!
THE BEATLES
THE ROLLING STONES

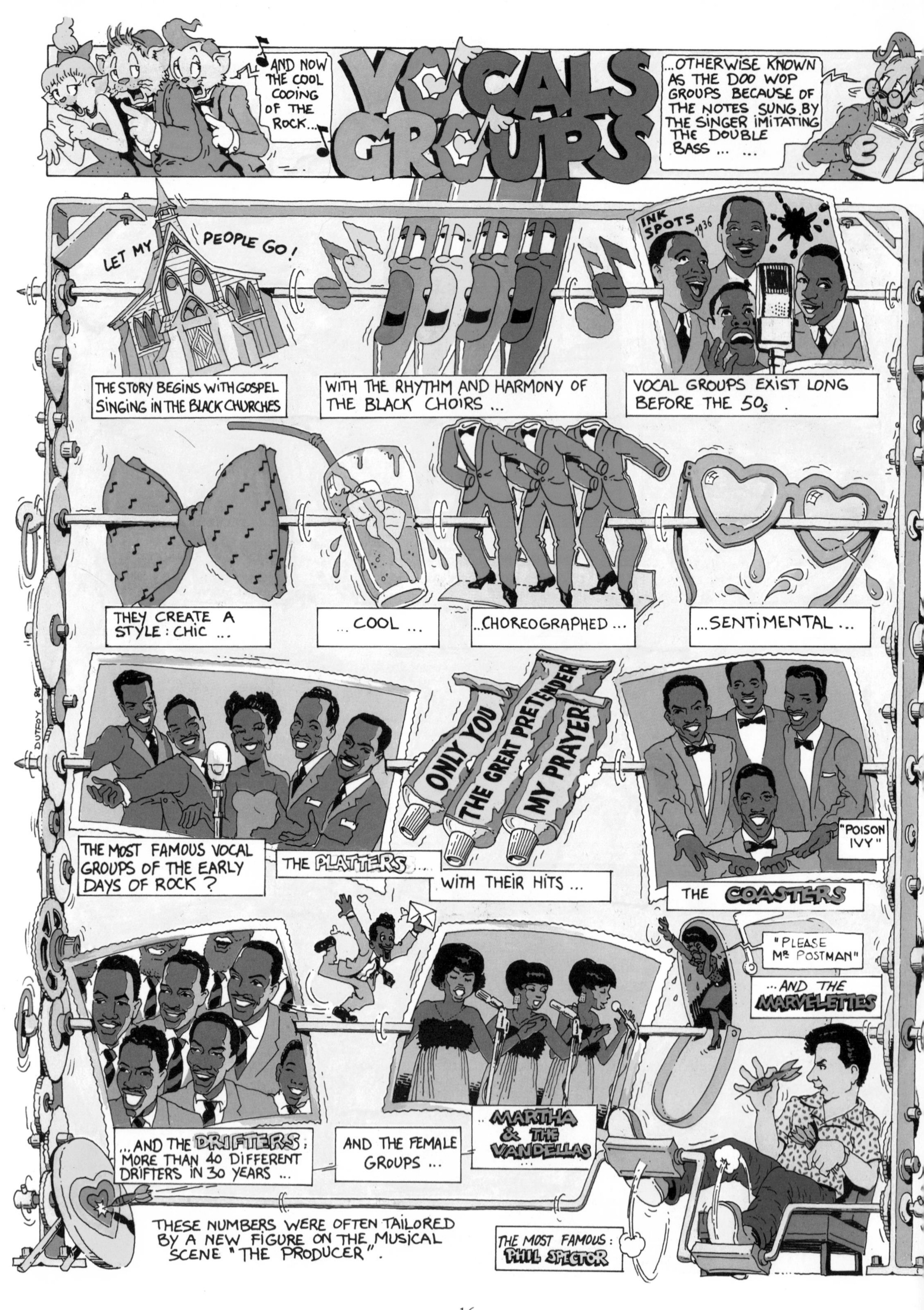
AND NOW THE COOL COOING OF THE ROCK...
VOCALS GROUPS
...OTHERWISE KNOWN AS THE DOO WOP GROUPS BECAUSE OF THE NOTES SUNG BY THE SINGER IMITATING THE DOUBLE BASS ... ...
LET MY PEOPLE GO!
INK SPOTS 1936
THE STORY BEGINS WITH GOSPEL SINGING IN THE BLACK CHURCHES
WITH THE RHYTHM AND HARMONY OF THE BLACK CHOIRS ...
VOCAL GROUPS EXIST LONG BEFORE THE 50s .
THEY CREATE A STYLE : CHIC ...
... COOL ...
...CHOREOGRAPHED ...
...SENTIMENTAL ...
THE MOST FAMOUS VOCAL GROUPS OF THE EARLY DAYS OF ROCK ?
THE PLATTERS ...
ONLY YOU
THE GREAT PRETENDER
MY PRAYER
WITH THEIR HITS ...
"POISON IVY"
THE COASTERS
...AND THE DRIFTERS ; MORE THAN 40 DIFFERENT DRIFTERS IN 30 YEARS ...
AND THE FEMALE GROUPS ...
... MARTHA & THE VANDELLAS ...
"PLEASE MR POSTMAN"
... AND THE MARVELETTES
THESE NUMBERS WERE OFTEN TAILORED BY A NEW FIGURE ON THE MUSICAL SCENE "THE PRODUCER".
THE MOST FAMOUS : PHIL SPECTOR

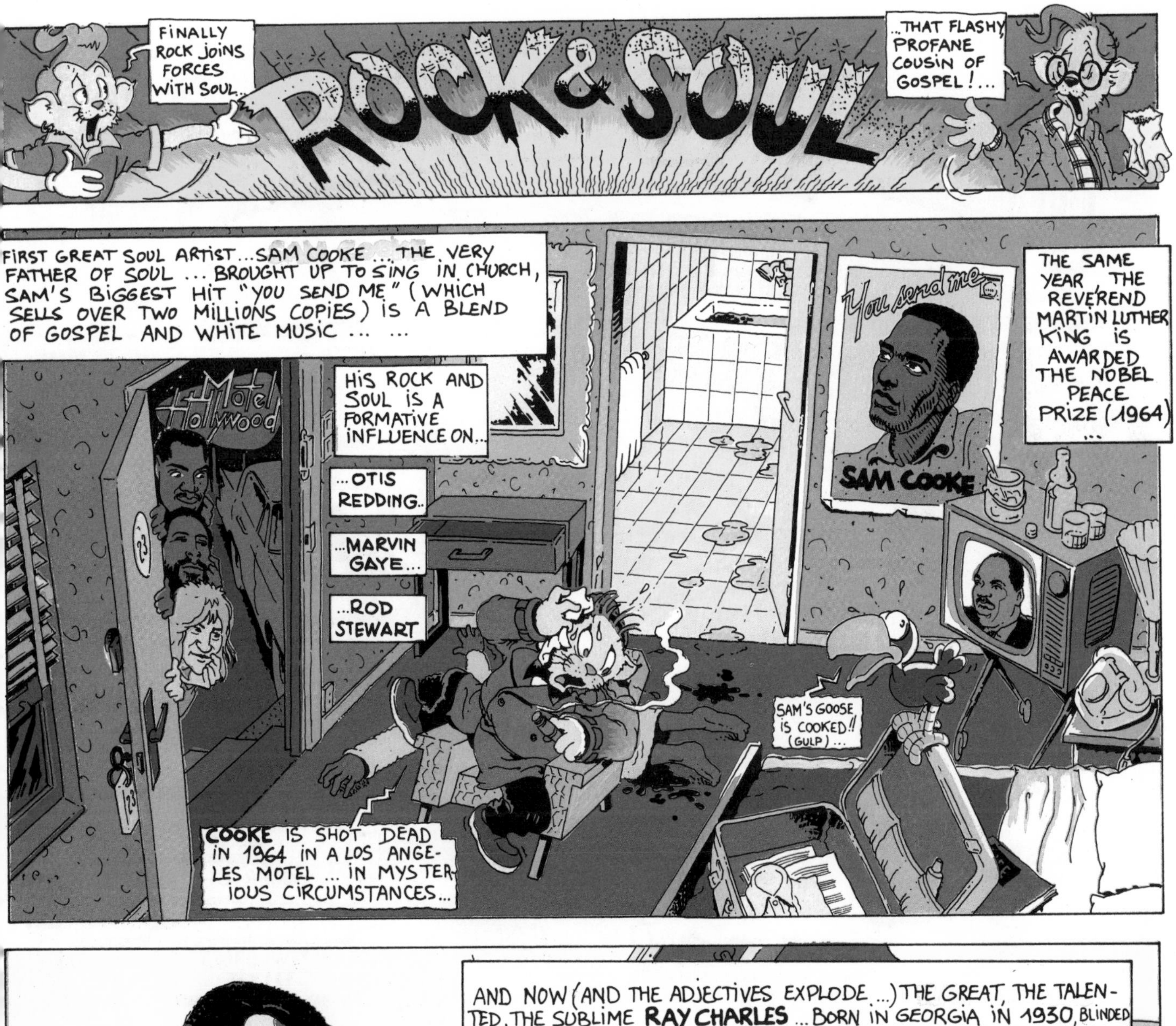

FIRST GREAT SOUL ARTIST...SAM COOKE... THE VERY FATHER OF SOUL... BROUGHT UP TO SING IN CHURCH, SAM'S BIGGEST HIT "YOU SEND ME" (WHICH SELLS OVER TWO MILLIONS COPIES) IS A BLEND OF GOSPEL AND WHITE MUSIC... ...

THE SAME YEAR, THE REVEREND MARTIN LUTHER KING IS AWARDED THE NOBEL PEACE PRIZE (1964)...

Motel Hollywood

HIS ROCK AND SOUL IS A FORMATIVE INFLUENCE ON...

...OTIS REDDING...

...MARVIN GAYE...

...ROD STEWART

You send me

SAM COOKE

SAM'S GOOSE IS COOKED!! (GULP)...

COOKE IS SHOT DEAD IN **1964** IN A LOS ANGELES MOTEL... IN MYSTERIOUS CIRCUMSTANCES...

AND NOW (AND THE ADJECTIVES EXPLODE...) THE GREAT, THE TALENTED, THE SUBLIME **RAY CHARLES**... BORN IN GEORGIA IN 1930, BLINDED AT THE AGE OF 6.... HIS MUSIC OPENS UP NEW AVENUES FOR ROCK... HE IS, FOR EXAMPLE, ONE OF THE PRECURSORS OF FUNK...

"WHAT 'D I SAY" IN 1959 COMBINES ALL THE INGREDIENTS OF A MUSICAL COCKTAIL MOLOTOV... GOSPEL, BLUES, SOUL AND ROCK!...

??? GOSP...!!

HANG ON COOKIE... AND TURN OVER!

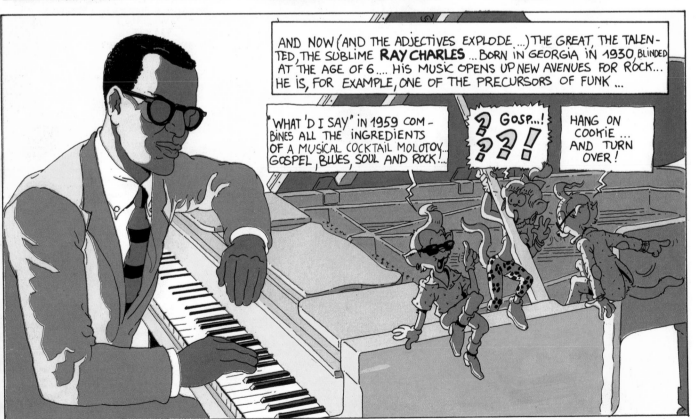

The Rocktail bar
BO DIDDLEY
AND NOW FOR THE SECRET INGREDIENTS OF THE FAMOUS ROCKTAIL:
A SPLASH OF POP ...
A DASH OF R & B (RHYTHM 'N' BLUES) BLACK AND STRONG ...
SEVERAL TOTS OF (ORIGINAL RECIPE) C & W (COUNTRY & WESTERN) ...
A SMALL MEASURE OF SACRAMENTAL WINE FROM A BLACK CHURCH... GOSPEL ...
A JIGGER OF JAZZ ...
A SPOT OF SOUL ...
A FEW DROPS OF DIXIE ...
HUHUM! HOW UTTERLY REPULSIVE.
CHUCK BERRY
DOO WOP DOO WOP SHOO BI DOO WOP
RAY CHARLES
ONE MORE TIME!
BILL HALEY
THEN SHAKE RATTLE 'N' ROLL !!! AND SERVE ...
LITTLE RICHARD
BUDDY HOLLY
EDDIE COCHRAN
JERRY LEE LEWIS
FATS DOMINO
PATIENCE FANS ... PATIENCE ...
ELVIS PRESLEY
EVERLY BROS.
HOW DO YOU LIKE THE ROCKTAIL COOKIE?
MINDBLOWING
SWWAHAASS!
GENE VINCENT
CARL PERKINS

BUT THE SUDDEN, UNIVERSAL SUCCESS OF ROCK IS NOT JUST A QUESTION OF TALENT ... ...

... IT'S ALSO DUE TO RADIO PROMOTION ... ...
ROCK

..und Roll

ENTER THE DISC JOCKEY ! ... (WHOOPS).

THE FIRST GREAT ROCK DISC JOCKEY IS ALAN FREED . THE FIRST TO PLAY BLACK MUSIC TO A WHITE PUBLIC , THE FIRST TO POPULARIZE THE WORDS ... ...
"ROCK'N'ROLL"
THE MOON DOG ROCK'N'ROLL HOUSE PARTY

MORALS

... THE SUCCESS OF HIS SHOW ALARMS THE ESTABLISHMENT DISGUSTED BY A MUSIC WHICH PREACHES PROMISCUITY, IDLENESS , INSTANT GRATIFICATION ... ...
BUT NOT YET POLITICS ! ...
BLURP
CLIC
MARX

THE ETYMOLOGY OF THE WORD ROCK'N' ROLL ...
LET'S ROCK, Mr BIRD ?
I'VE JUST

WHICH ONE MIGHT ERRONEOUSLY BELIEVE TO BE NAUTICAL ...
IRONED MY FEATHERS
HELP!

IS TO BE FOUND IN ... ER ... EUPHEMISTIC REFERENCES HUM ...
?

AMONGST THE BLACK POPULATION OF THE U.S.A. ... TO ... ER . FORNIC ... ER ... THE ACT OF ER
HUHUM

... SEX ... ! ...
WWWAAOOOH

COOKIE
GULP

AND THERE YOU HAVE IT CATS - WE REACH THE END OF THE BEGINNINGS OF ROCK...
HUMRRH !...
YOU'RE SO CLEVER CAT!...
ROCK! ROCK! THEY THINK OF NOTHING BUT ROCK!

BUT AROUND 1958... ROCK RUNS OUT OF STEAM ...
!
OBVIOUSLY!...
?!

COCHRAN AND HOLLY ARE DEAD, BERRY IS IN PRISON, LITTLE RICHARD HAS GIVEN UP ROCK FOR RELIGION. LEWIS IS BANNED.
HE JUST NEVER STOPS

WE ARE SOON TO WITNESS ... THE DUBIOUS PRACTICE OF PAYOLA ...
BLABBERMOUTH ! ! ...

I BEG YOUR PARDON! THERE ARE ALREADY TOO MANY PICTURES IN THIS BOOK. WE NEED MORE TEXT, MORE ANALYSIS ...

MORE ELVIS ?...
AH ... PEACE AND THE PASTORAL

HANG ON COOKIE, I'VE JUST FINISHED ... CHAPTER 2...
YOU'RE A DRAG EGGHEAD !...

THE BOSS!
DDRRIIIIINNG

YES Mr VAN DER PLOOK ... NO, Mr VAN DER PLOOK ... THE FIRST CHAPTER IS FINISHED Mr VAN DER PLOOK ... OF COURSE Mr VAN DER PLOOK ... GOODBYE Mr VAN DER PLOOK ... PHEW
WORK
CONCENTRATION
SWEAT
TAK TAK
TAK TAK TAK

PHEW !

O.K. TEAM! FEET UP! ENOUGH ROCK FOR TODAY! LET'S TAKE A BREAK!...
RAYMOND'S RIGHT!...

ROCK ROCK ROCK EVERYBODY
MURMF
TINK
TINK
Drink CHEER UP

TEEN IDOLS
$
ADORATION
I ♥ YOU RICKY BOBBY PAT TAB
I'M A FAN
KISS ME
PLEASE LOVE ME
SIGH!
I NEED YOU
HERE I COME

AT THE END OF THE 50's ROCK - ANTI-SOCIAL ROCK - SUDDENLY MEANS 'BIG MONEY... ...

2. THEN RE-HEAT A FEW TIRED OLD THEMES, ADDING A DASH OF ROCK RELISH · HIGH SCHOOL : HOT RODS, DANCES, BOBBYSOCKS, FLIRTS, TEARS, PONY TAILS ... ...
CLASS OF '60
BOBBY VINTON Roses are red
PAUL ANKA Diana
PAT BOONE Ain't that a shame
LESLIE GORE It's my party
FRANKIE AVALON Venus
RICKY NELSON Poor little fool
BRENDA LEE I'm sorry
FABIAN Turn me loose
CURTIS LEE Pretty little angel eyes
TOMMY SANDS Teenage crush
BOBBY DARIN Dream Lover
Bobby Vinton
Leslie Gore
Paul Anka
Pat Boone
Frankie Avalon
Tommy Sands
Curtis Lee
Bobby Darin
ROCK
RICKY
POP CORN
Ricky Nelson
Brenda Lee
Fabian
FIDEL CASTRO
...INSULAR PREOCCUPATIONS AT A TIME WHEN THE WORLD OUTSIDE BEGINS TO LOOM: IN 1959, FIDEL CASTRO DRIVES BATISTA (THE DICTATOR) OUT OF CUBA ... ...
3. NEXT CREATE A CULT BY MEANS OF FAN CLUBS, FAN MAIL, FAN MAGS ... ...
Teen
R·N·R
T.V. STARS
HI KIDS
Hello Rock
FAN'S FUN
4. FINALLY LAUNCH ON AN EAGER WORLD THE PRODUCT WHICH IS...
EXIT
NOT MADE TO LAST ! ...

... BUT (OVER ZEALOUS) MARKETING = (SOMETIMES) CORRUPTION !!! ...
Daily Scandal
... IN 1960, THE PRESS EXPOSES THE DIRTY DEALINGS OF ... ...
PAYOLA!
2 DISC-JOCKEYS SUSPECTED!!!
FATHER OF R'N'R!
D.J. Alan FREED
Yesterday scandal broke out in the music industry! Two leading disc jockeys are to be investigated. One the famous Alan Freed some-times Known as the "Father of Rock and Roll" the other the all-american clean-living, Dick Clark presenter of "American Bandstand"
THE MUSIC INDUSTRY PUTS THE DJ AT THE CROSSROADS - HE'S PRESSURISED BY THE RADIO NETWORKS, BY THE RECORD COMPANIES ... AND BY HIS OWN AMBITION ...
D.J. Dick CLARK
... ODD? THIS SUDDEN DESIRE TO. PURGE ROCK? NOT AT ALL ... SOME POLITICIANS CLAIM THAT ROCK WAS INVENTED BY THE RUSSIANS TO CORRUPT AMERICAN YOUTH !! ...
ROCK
ROLL
WARFSKI! WARFSKI!
RESULTS OF THE INVESTIGATION! CLARK IS CLEARED ...
SKLONK SKLONK
FREED, ACCUSED OF ILLEGALLY RECEIVING $ 30650, IS FOUND GUILTY, AND DIES IN 1965, A VICTIM OF ALCOHOL AND ... INJUSTICE.
IF ... THE BEGINNINGS OF ROCK = TALENT AND ... TEEN IDOLS = CASH ... OUR NEXT CHAPTER = THE MARRIAGE OF CASH AND TALENT !!!

THE RISE AND FALL
OF
ELVIS THE KING
COL PARKER
IN 5 ACTS ...
PEANUT BUTTER
ELViiiiis...

ACT I
EARLY DAYS

THE FABULOUS STORY OF ELVIS BEGINS (MORE OR LESS) LIKE THIS...

JULY 5TH 1954 IN SAM PHILLIPS' SUN STUDIO IN MEMPHIS ... ...
SUN
RECORD COM
... A SAM SESSION ...

... AN UNKNOWN TRUCK DRIVER RECORDS A BALLAD ...
SYRUP SUGAR HONEY

SUDDENLY A DIFFERENT SOUND COMES FROM THE STUDIO
!?

... A MUSIC WHICH EXCITES ... WHICH ...
$ $
TITILLATES HIS BUSINESS ACUMEN

SAM MUST TRACK IT DOWN ...

WHO IS THIS WHITE ROCKER WHO SINGS WITH "SOUL ?!"

WHAT'S GOING ON ?!?

JUST FOOLING AROUND BETWEEN TAKES, MR PHILLIPS ... SORRY ...

DON'T...
DON'T STOP YOUNG MAN GO ON ! ...

... AND SO BEGINS THE CAREER OF ELVIS ...

IN FACT, IT ALL BEGAN A LONG TIME BEFORE ... WHEN HE WAS SMALL, ELVIS LONGED FOR A BIKE ... BUT $ 55 WAS TOO MUCH FOR HIS PARENTS ...
$55
$ 12.95

SO THEY BUY HIM A GUITAR FOR $ 12.95 ...
SIGH...
... SOME INVESTMENT ! ...

BUT IN TRUTH, THE STORY REALLY BEGINS WITH THE ARRIVAL IN ELVIS'S LIFE OF HIS SHREWD MANAGER ...
25%
... COLONEL PARKER, PART BARNUM, PART W.C. FIELDS, ... PART MACHIAVELLI ...

ACT II
FAME AT LAST
UNDER PARKER'S DIRECTION, ELVIS HITS THE NATION... ... JANUARY 28TH, 1956... ... IT'S RAINING OUTSIDE... ...
BUT BOY!...ON THE T.V. SCREEN, IS IT HOT ELVIS SINGS... AND AMERICA TREMBLES
Heartbreak
HOTEL
HOTEL
TBREAK ST
SCANDALOUS!! DISGUSTING!! (NEW YORK TIMES)!!! STRIPTEASE FULLY CLOTHED (SAN FRANCISCO CHRONICLE)!! ELVIS THE PELVIS!

ACT III
THE KING.

"HEARTBREAK HOTEL" (FAST Nº 1 IN THE CHARTS) SUMS UP THE PRESLEY FORMULA
A SIMPLE SENTIMENTAL TEXT (WOMAN'S INFIDELITY)...
+ ELVIS'S SULKY BROODY BLUESY VOICE...
+ HIS OVERTLY SEXUAL STAGE PRESENCE!
HELP
FREUD
THE NATIONAL LIBIDO SURRENDERS!...

HIS EARLY HITS * ARE NOW LEGENDS ... ...
MARTHA! MY FAVORITE RECORD !!!
ELVIS
ELVIS PRESLEY HOUND DOG

YOUR MIND'S GONE ELMER ... IT WAS ALL SHOOK UP!!
WITH THE FAMOUS SOB HAAAAAA...
Elvis

JAILHOUSE ROCK
ELVIS FAN CLUB

* OFTEN THE WORK OF COMPOSERS LEIBER & STOLLER
JAILHOUSE ROCK
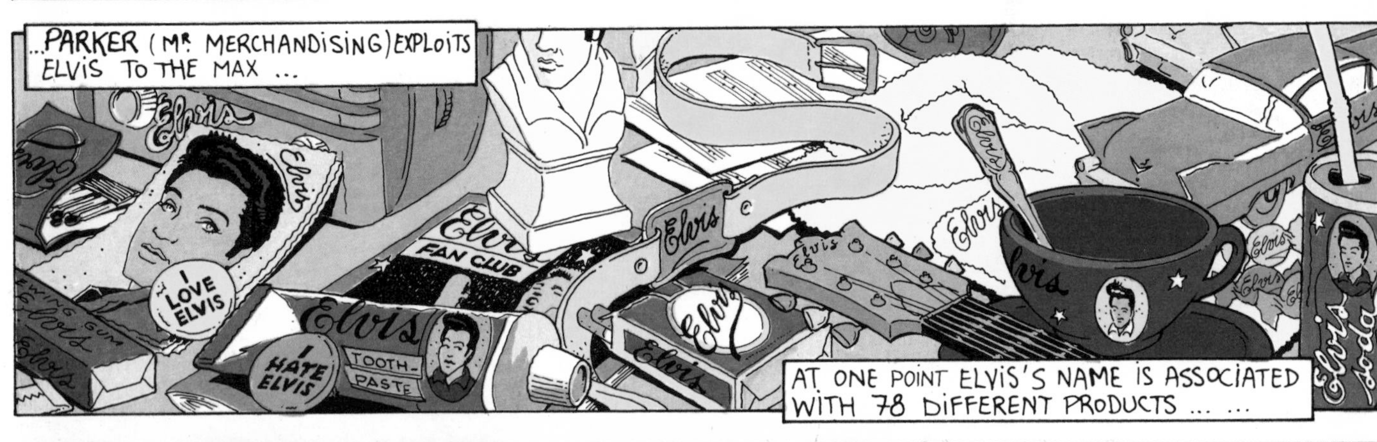
...PARKER (MR MERCHANDISING) EXPLOITS ELVIS TO THE MAX ...
Elvis
ELVIS FAN CLUB
I LOVE ELVIS
I HATE ELVIS
Elvis TOOTH-PASTE
CHEWING GUM
Elvis soda
AT ONE POINT ELVIS'S NAME IS ASSOCIATED WITH 78 DIFFERENT PRODUCTS ... ...
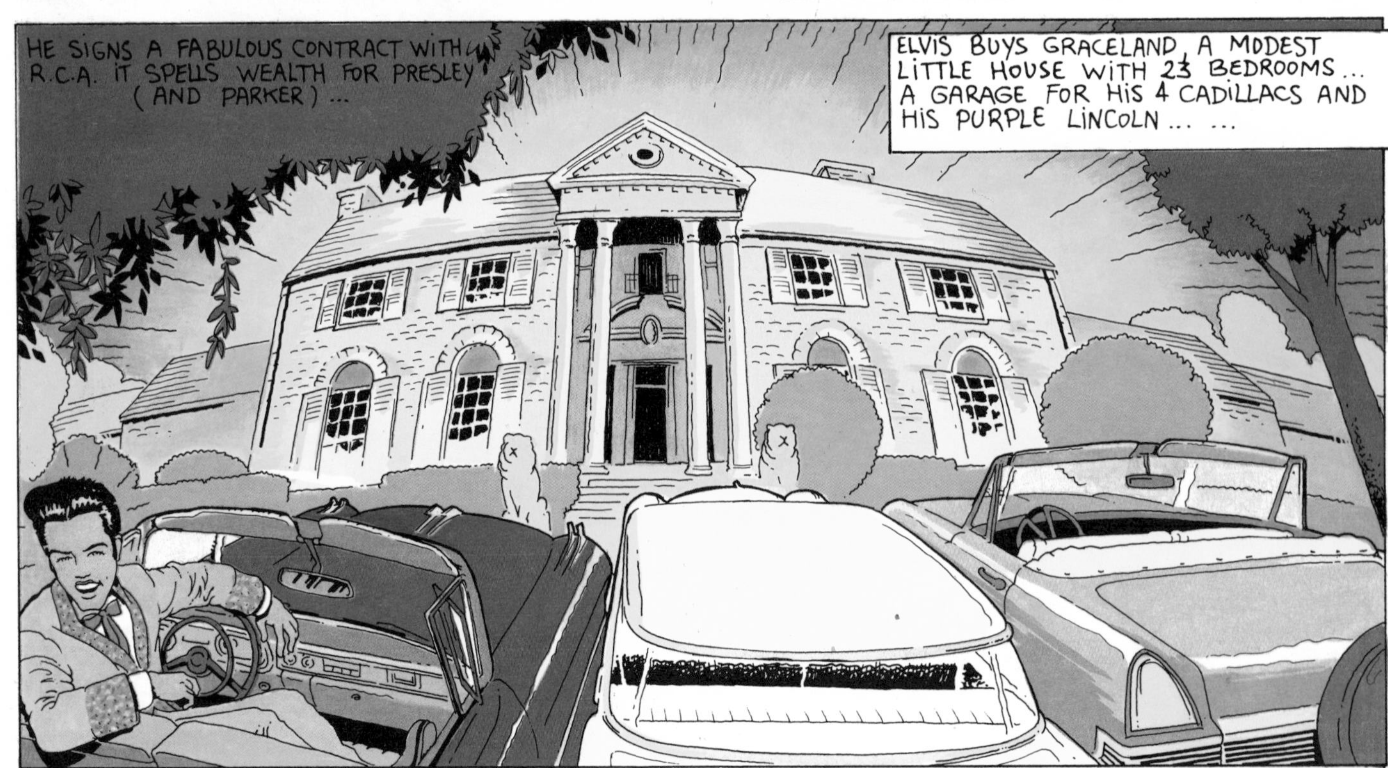
HE SIGNS A FABULOUS CONTRACT WITH R.C.A. IT SPELLS WEALTH FOR PRESLEY (AND PARKER) ...
ELVIS BUYS GRACELAND, A MODEST LITTLE HOUSE WITH 23 BEDROOMS ... A GARAGE FOR HIS 4 CADILLACS AND HIS PURPLE LINCOLN ... ...

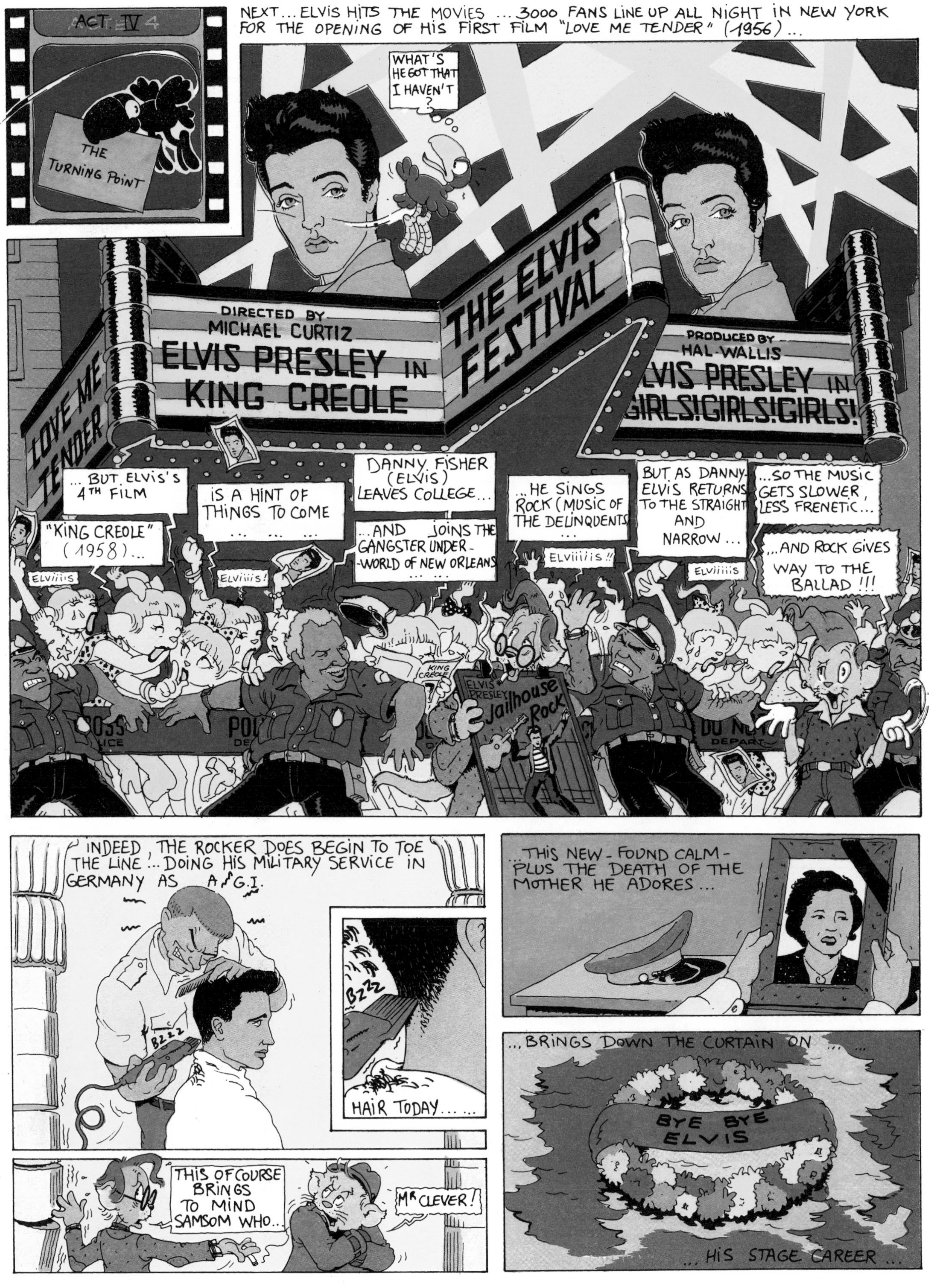

ACT IV

THE TURNING POINT

NEXT... ELVIS HITS THE MOVIES ... 3000 FANS LINE UP ALL NIGHT IN NEW YORK FOR THE OPENING OF HIS FIRST FILM "LOVE ME TENDER" (1956)...

WHAT'S HE GOT THAT I HAVEN'T ?

THE ELVIS FESTIVAL

LOVE ME TENDER

DIRECTED BY MICHAEL CURTIZ
ELVIS PRESLEY IN KING CREOLE

PRODUCED BY HAL WALLIS
ELVIS PRESLEY IN GIRLS! GIRLS! GIRLS!

... BUT ELVIS'S 4TH FILM

"KING CREOLE" (1958)...

IS A HINT OF THINGS TO COME ... ...

DANNY FISHER (ELVIS) LEAVES COLLEGE...

... AND JOINS THE GANGSTER UNDER-WORLD OF NEW ORLEANS ... ...

... HE SINGS ROCK (MUSIC OF THE DELINQUENTS) ...

BUT AS DANNY-ELVIS RETURNS TO THE STRAIGHT AND NARROW ...

... SO THE MUSIC GETS SLOWER, LESS FRENETIC...

... AND ROCK GIVES WAY TO THE BALLAD !!!

Elviiiis

Elviiiis!

Elviiiis !!

Elviiiiis

KING CREOLE

ELVIS PRESLEY Jailhouse Rock

POLICE DEPARTMENT

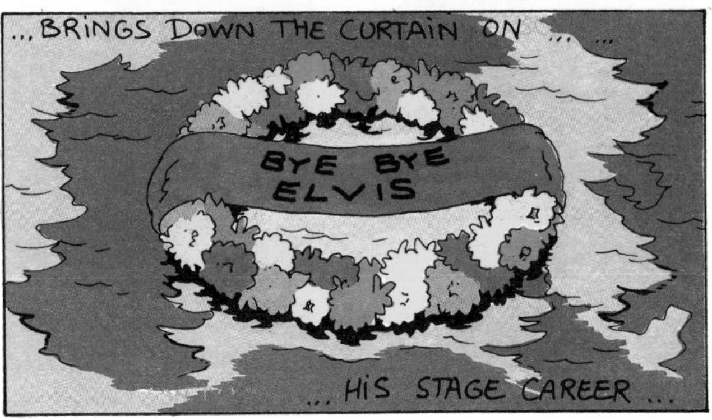

ACT V
DECLINE AND FALL
CHUTE

GRACELAND, THE RETREAT.

ELVIiiiiS...
... GIRLS ...

... BOOZE ...

... NOT EVEN ADMIRATION...

PEANUT BUTTER
... CAN STOP THE DECLINE...

SOMETIMES LONELINESS WEIGHS HEAVY... IN HOLLYWOOD, ON SUNSET BOU LEVARD, HE TAKES OFF HIS DARK GLASSES...
... BUT NO ONE RECOGNISES HIM...

INTERNATIONAL
ELVIS
AROUND THE CLOCK
HE MAKES A SERIES OF COME-BACKS AT LAS VEGAS.

... DOES A T.V. SPECIAL WITH FRANK SINATRA ...
MY WAY
... WHO ONCE SAID THAT "ROCK IS A MUSIC FOR HALF-WITS"!!

LOVE ME TENDER
... BUT ELVIS HAS CHANGED..

ELVIS AARON PRESLEY
JANUARY 8, 1935
AUGUST 16, 1977
... AND DEATH IS WAITING IN THE WINGS ... ...

GLOOM...
SNIF
HRRRNNF
SNIIIF
ONCE MORE WITH FEELING ...
CHIN UP COOKIE...
ELVIIIIIIISNIIF
SNIIF
SNIIF
ELVIS
Elvis Presley
FUNERAL MARCH
* EXIT ELVIS...

BUT...
WE'RE CRAZY!
SNIF
SNIF

ELVIS ISN'T DEAD!
WHAT ?!
HOW'S THAT?

...OUR HISTORY OF ROCK HAS ONLY REACHED 1960 ...
?
!

SO...
ELVIS LIVES !!
YEAH
WAOO

SMACK
GULP!

THE DAWN OF A NEW ERA...
1960

TIME PASSES SO FAST... ... GLOOM ...

IN THE U.S.A., PURE ROCK GIVES WAY TO A NEW KIND OF ROCK ... IT'S THE (NEW) DANCE ERA ...
?!
OH NO, NOT AGAIN!
... ADIEU THE 50s

CHUBBY CHECKER LEAVES THE CHICKEN FARM WHERE HE WORKS AS A PLUCKER TO LAUNCH THE ...
TWIST!
TWIST!
TWIST AND SHOUT

YOU'RE NOBODY_ JUST NOBODY!_ IF YOU CAN'T DANCE...
THE LIMBO!...
... THE MADISON! ...

LEFT FOOT
FORWARD
RIGHT FOOT
FORWARD
PASS THE LEFT
FOOT BEHIND
BRING THE RIGHT
FOOT OVER
CROSS THE
LEFT FOOT
BRING THE RIGHT
FOOT OVER
BRING THE LEFT
FOOT OVER
BRING THE RIGHT
FOOT OVER
THEN, TAKING CARE NOT TO BREAK YOUR LEG!
!?
TWO JUMPS FORWARD ON THE FIRST BEAT OF THE TWO NEXT BARS...
WHICH TAKE YOU UNDER THE BAMBOO BAR...
LIMBO!...
START AGAIN WITH
THE FIRST STEP...

POST_LIMBO MAN
A KNOTTY PROBLEM!...

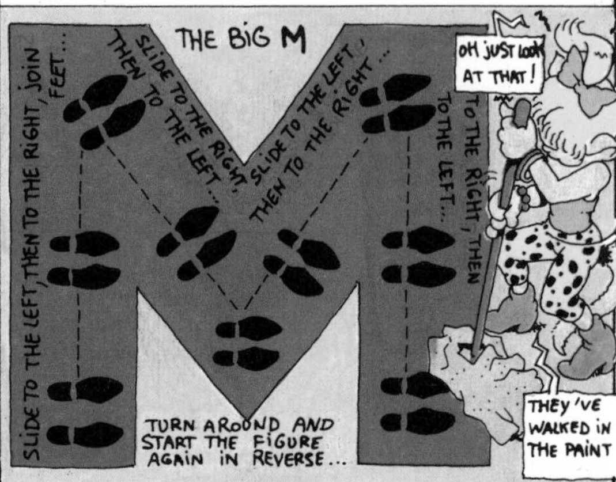
THE BIG M
SLIDE TO THE LEFT, THEN TO THE RIGHT, JOIN FEET...
SLIDE TO THE RIGHT, THEN TO THE LEFT...
SLIDE TO THE LEFT, THEN TO THE RIGHT...
TO THE RIGHT, THEN TO THE LEFT...
TURN AROUND AND START THE FIGURE AGAIN IN REVERSE...
OH JUST LOOK AT THAT!
THEY'VE WALKED IN THE PAINT

OR THE BUNNY HOP...

THE SWIM

THE CHICKEN

THE MONKEY

THE LOCOMOTION
TCHOO
TCHOO

THE BATMAN

...THE
CRASH

...IF ONE ... ANALYSES THE DANCE CRAZE, ONE NOTICES ... A DESIRE FOR COMPLEXITY ... AND AS A RESULT...
HEY COOKIE...

... AN ABS... ABSENCE OF PHYSICAL CONTACT ... A SIGN OF... ... IN_DI_VI_DU_A_LI_TY... NOT OF TIMIDITY ... ER ...
...WHAT HAVE YOU DONE...

...AND ONE GLIMPSES THE FIRST SIGNS OF A FASHION WHICH WILL EVENTUALLY BLOSSOM INTO THE BREAKDANCE AND THE SMURF...BUT... ... ...
... To ANDRE... ?!

...BUT WHILE AMERICA DANCES... AND GETS ITSELF UNTANGLED ... OTHER ROCKERS ELSEWHERE... ARE DOING NEW AND WONDERFUL THINGS ...
KAT AIR
GREAT! I LOVE FLYING!
ENGLAND, A SMALL ISLAND OFF THE COAST OF EUROPE IS...
KAT-AIR

YES MR VAN DER PLOOK... NO MR VAN DER PLOOK... WE'RE LEAVING RIGHT AWAY... ON A CHARTER FLIGHT - SECOND CLASS... WE'RE TAKING SANDWICHES...

BEATLES & Cie

TUT
TUT TUT
TIME
PASHES …
HIC
RAYMOND
PUT THAT
BOTTLE BACK!

MERSEY
MUSE
MELODY
Powder
GENIUS
TALENT
J
P
G
R

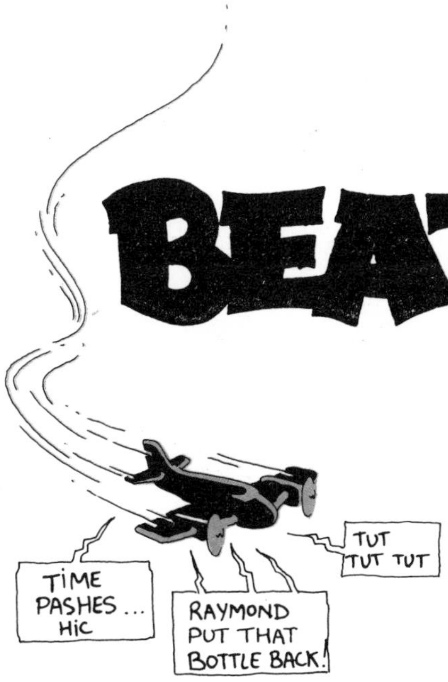

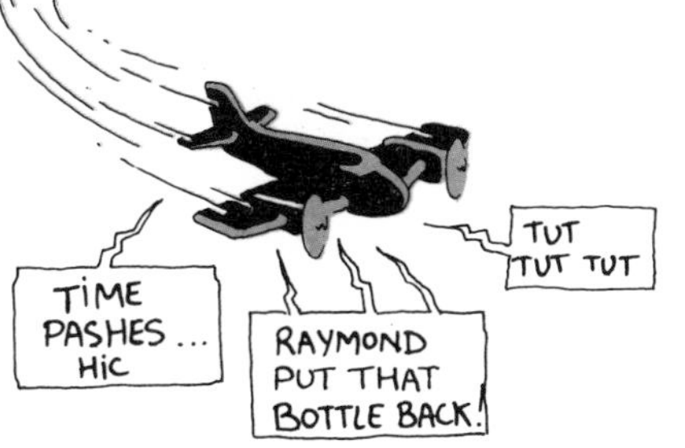

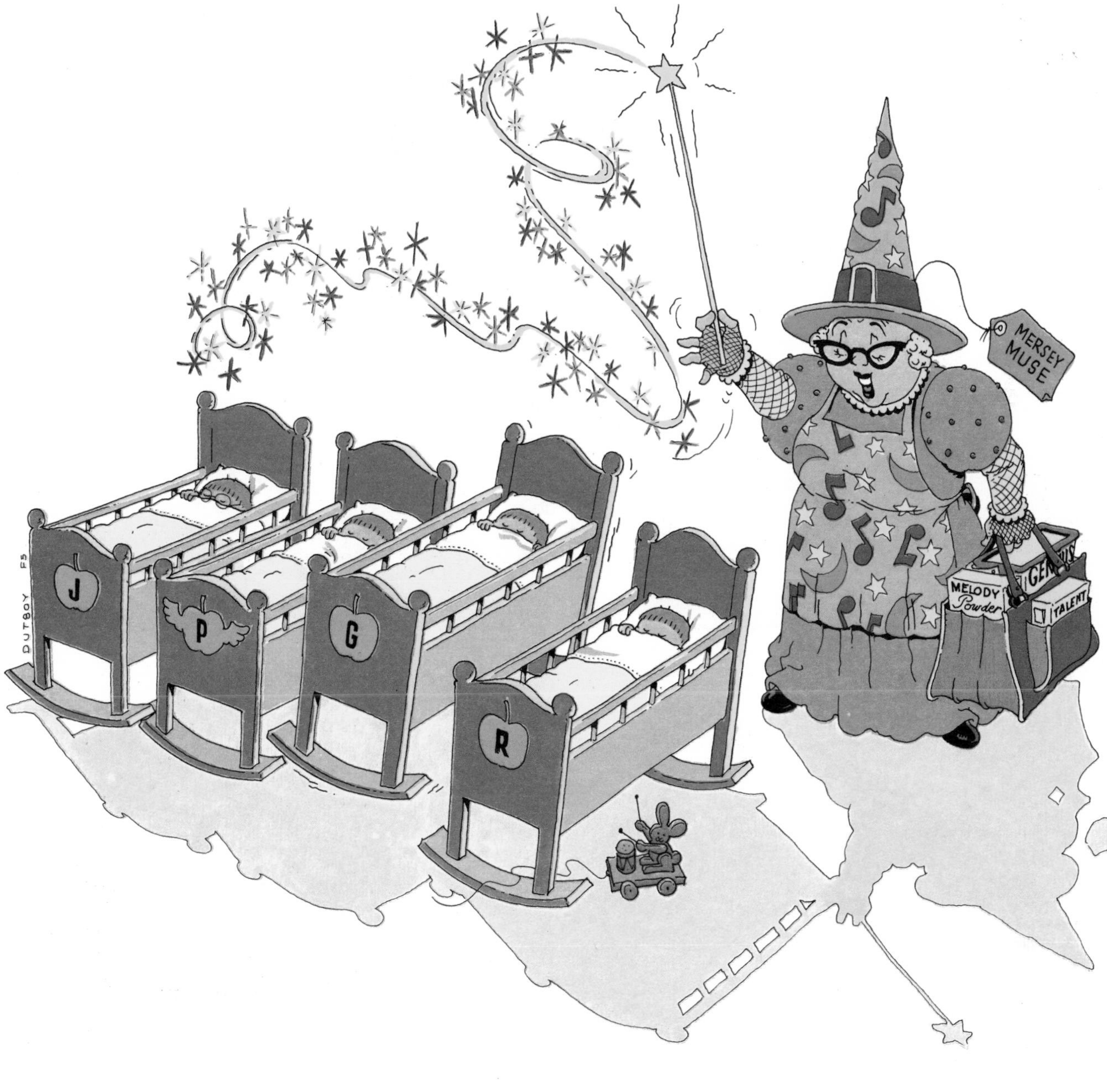

LONDON ... THE CALM BEFORE THE STORM ...
PUBLIC SUBWAY
UNDERGROUND
PUBLIC SUBWAY
GOD SAVE THE QUEEN
THE END OF THE 50s ... MY LOST YOUTH ... HIC ...
ODD TASTE THIS ... HIC ... BEER ...
RAYMOND...
OH TO BE IN ENGLAND! ...

WHERE A GENT MIGHT MEET A TEDDY BOY ...
?
HEAVENS!
... WHERE THE DARING FEW MIGHT QUIT THE TEA ROOM FOR A CAPUCCINO IN A COFFEE BAR ... ...
THE WILD SIDE MILDRED!

... BUT WHERE MUSIC IS NON-AGGRESSIVE - ...
SKIFFLE

A WATERED-DOWN FOLK-BLUES - WHAT LEADBELLY WOULD HAVE PLAYED IF HE'D DRUNK EARL GREY TEA ...

... SKIFFLE - LIKE PUNK LATER - IS A DO-IT-YOURSELF MUSIC. BANJO, WASHBOARD, MAKE-SHIFT BASS.
découpage

LONNIE DONEGAN LEAVES THE CHRIS BARBER 'TRAD' NEW ORLEANS BAND AND MAKES A HIT OF ... ...
ROCK ISLAND LINE (1956)

THEN ROCK HITS THE SCENE - THANKS TO A DISCOVERY OF LARRY PARNES AND JOHN KENNEDY - ...
ONE ... TOMMY HICKS OR ...
TOMMY STEELE

ROCK WITH THE CAVEMAN* (1956)
* STONEAGE ... ROCK ... LOGICAL! ...

EVEN THE B.B.C. "SWITCHES ON" - PRESENTING THIS "BARBARIC" MUSIC IN THE SHOWCASE ... ...
6.5 SPECIAL

TIN PAN ALLEY STARTS TO TURN OUT REPLICAS OF ELVIS

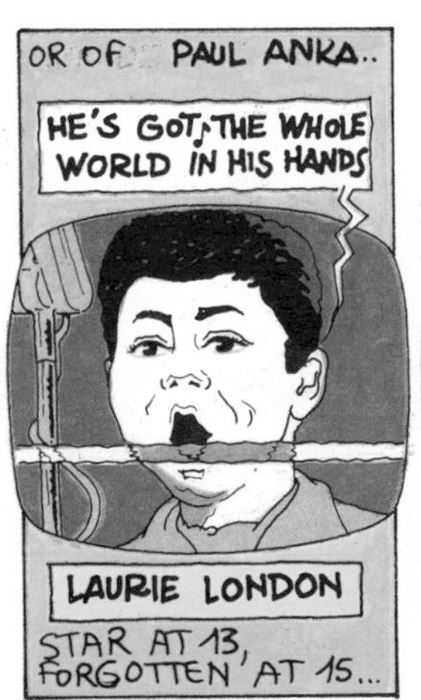

SEXY

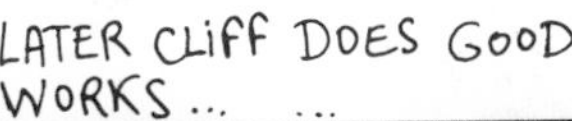

AND NOW CATS ... IN THE FAIRY GROTTO... ... ...

...THE MAGIC BOOK...
Beatles
OF THE STORY THAT BEGINS ...

...ON THE BANKS OF THE MERSEY...
Mersey River

...IN LIVERPOOL...

SHIPS ARRIVE FROM AMERICA ...
CUNARD
LINES

... BRINGING ROCK MUSIC WHICH INSPIRES... AMONG OTHERS ...

THE QUARRYMEN
...A GROUP, HALF-SKIFFLE, HALF-ROCK, COMPOSED OF...

JOHN LENNON, CLOWN AND EXTROVERT

PAUL McCARTNEY, SHY AND POETIC ...

...THE THIRD IS CHOSEN BECAUSE HIS MOTHER PUTS UP WITH RE-HEARSALS IN HER HOUSE

GEORGE HARRISON CLEAN-CUT BUT MYSTICAL

IN SEARCH OF A NAME ...

Johnny and the Moondogs ?? The Silver Beatles

...AND FAME ...THE GROUP PLAYS THE CLUBS IN HAMBURG .
STRIP
Star-Club
TOP TEN

AFTER THE DEATH OF STU SUTCLIFFE ...

AND THE DISMISSAL OF PETE BEST

THEY LOOK FOR A DRUMMER
?
AND DISCOVER

...RINGO STARR, LOONEY BUT HOMELY...

THE BEATLES ARE BORN !

RETURNING TO LIVERPOOL...

...THEY PLAY AT THE
cavern
...WHERE THEY ATTRACT THE AT-TENTION OF A FAILED ACTOR...

?

...BRIAN EPSTEIN, THEIR FUTURE MANAGER

FINAL INGRE-DIENT : A SHREWD PRODUCER-ARRANGER ...

...GEORGE MARTIN (THE 5TH BEATLE ?)

EVERYTHING'S IN PLACE!

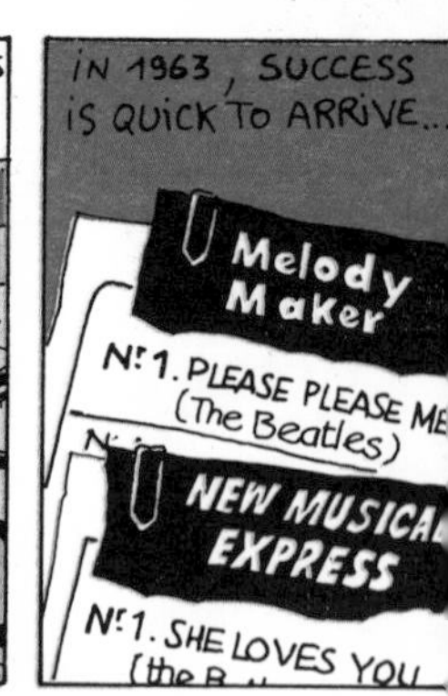
IN 1963, SUCCESS IS QUICK TO ARRIVE...
Melody Maker
Nº1. PLEASE PLEASE ME (The Beatles)
NEW MUSICAL EXPRESS
Nº1. SHE LOVES YOU

JOHN
GEORGE
RINGO
PAUL

OCTOBER '63 ! ROYAL BLESSING ! THEY PERFORM BEFORE THE QUEEN ...

EVEN "THE TIMES" AP-PROVES OF THE BEATLES.
TIMES
...SPEAKING OF AEOLIAN CADENCES IN "NOT A SECOND TIME" WHICH IT COMPARES WITH MAHLER'S "SONG OF THE EARTH"...

1964 AFTER THE U. K... THE U. S. A .
JOHN
GEORGE
PAUL
RINGO

APRIL 4TH 1964, THEIR RECORDS ARE 1, 2, 3, 4, 5, ON THE AMER-ICAN HIT PARADE...
THE BEATLES

NEXT STEP ? THE CINEMA... WITH " A HARD DAY'S NIGHT ".
A FACT AND FICTION STORY OF THEIR CRAZY TOURS. (1964)

... THEN A WORLD TOUR ... ...

... AND ANOTHER FILM: " HELP " (1965)
THEY GET MEDALS FROM THE QUEEN. (A FAN!).
MBE
MBE
MBE
MBE

... BUT FATIGUE AND STRAIN ALREADY SHOW ON THE SLEEVE OF...
BEATLES FOR SALE
stéréo
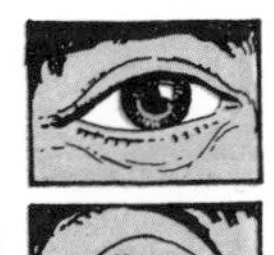
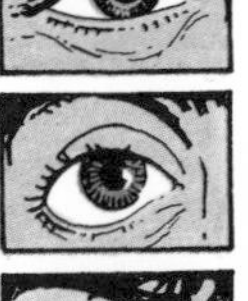

EVEN THEIR MUSIC REFLECTS THE CHANGE - MORE CYNICAL, LESS BUBBLY ...
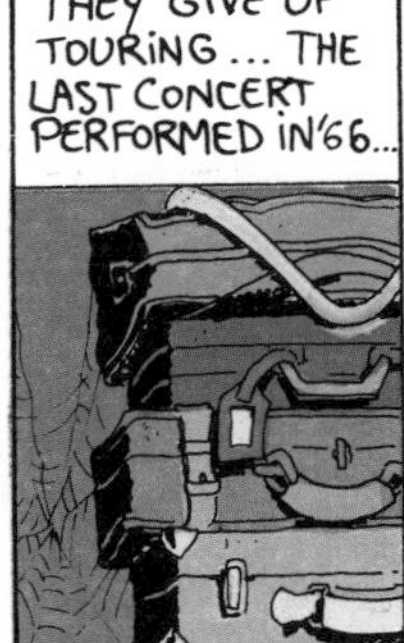
THEY GIVE UP TOURING ... THE LAST CONCERT PERFORMED IN '66...

THEIR MUSIC BECOMES MORE COMPLEX ...
RUBBER SOUL
REVOLVER

... A COMPLEXITY ACCENTUATED BY DRUGS ...

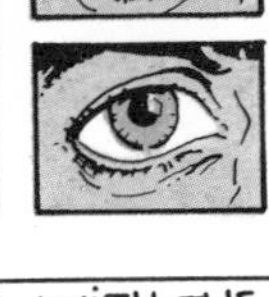

JOHN IS INFLUENCED BY BOB DYLAN ...

ROCK ATTAINS GREATNESS WITH THE FIRST "CONCEPT" ALBUM (1967).
WE'RE CLEVER BOYS ...

Sgt PEPPERS LONELY HEARTS CLUB BAND
A REVOLUTION ...

... FOLLOWED BY A REVOLUTION IN THEIR LIVES...
IN SEARCH OF LOVE, THE BEATLES JOIN UP WITH ...

... THE MAHARISHI MAHESH YOGI

BUT PARADISE HAS A BITTER TASTE...

BRIAN EPSTEIN DIES (1967)...

A HIPPY ENTERPRISE FLOPS ...
MAGICAL MYSTERY TOUR

THE MAHARISHI IS TOO FOND OF WOMEN ...

AND RINGO CAN'T TAKE THE EXOTIC FOOD ...
BEURK CURRY

"APPLE" THEIR COMPANY WHICH MARRIES PHILANTHROPY AND CAPITALISM...,

... HAS PROBLEMS!...
BURP

THE GROUP SPLITS ...
YOKO ONO
LINDA
THE BEATLES MARRY AND RE-MARRY ...

ON "ABBEY ROAD" THEY CROSS THEIR LAST STREET TOGETHER.

... AND "LET IT BE" (1969) IS THEIR SWAN SONG ...

THE BEATLES ARE A PHENOMENON OF THE 60s ... ...
DRIIIINNG!
69
70
71

... BUT WE HAVEN'T FINISHED YET CATS!

STILL ONE MORE!...
MAGICAL MYSTERY DOOR

HICCUP... WHAT A P.P.P. RETTY PICKSHER ...VERY PRETTY... HIC...
WELCOME TO THE MAGIC WORLD OF BEATLE MUSIC...
AND NOW... OUR COMPETITION! GUESS THE TITLES...
COME OFF IT FAIRY!
AT LAST... AN OPPORTUNITY TO USE OUR INTELLIGENCE!

Lucy in
MAXWELL
PENNY LANE
CIRCUS
FOR THE BENEFIT OF
REVOLUTIO
MAGICAL MYSTERY DOOR
HIPS!
ANOTHER DOOR ??
THIS PLACE IS AS COMPLEX AS LENNON'S MIND!

I FOUND Z (HIC)

CHILDSPLAY

① HELTER SKELTER ② THE LONG AND WINDING ROAD ③ LUCY IN THE SKY WITH DIAMONDS ④ GOOD DAY SUNSHINE ⑤ NORWEGIAN WOOD ⑥ I WANT TO HOLD YOUR HAND ⑦ TICKET TO RIDE ⑧ ONE AFTER 909 ⑨ SHE'S LEAVING HOME ⑩ MAXWELL'S SILVER HAMMER ⑪ RAIN ⑫ ELEANOR RIGBY ⑬ SGT PEPPER'S LONELY HEARTS CLUB BAND ⑭ PENNY LANE ⑮ WOMAN ⑯ FLYING ⑰ FOR THE BENEFIT OF MR KITE ⑱ STRAWBERRY FIELDS FOR EVER ⑲ COLD TURKEY ⑳ PIGGIES ㉑ HELP ㉒ REVOLUTION ㉓ I AM ONLY SLEEPING ㉔ FIXING A HOLE ㉕ BIRTHDAY ㉖ BLACKBIRD ㉗ YELLOW SUBMARINE ㉘ I'M THE WALRUS ㉙ HER MAJESTY ㉚ DRIVE MY CAR ㉛ DR ROBERT ㉜ CARRY THAT WEIGHT ㉝ OCTOPUS'S GARDEN

IT'S A GIVE-AWAY

NASTY THAT ONE

FANTASTIC OUTPUT ! 230 SONGS BETWEEN 1962 AND 1967... GREATEST SUCCESS ! "YESTERDAY"...

(WHICH THEY CALL "SCRAMBLED EGGS") SELLS MORE THAN 8 MILLIONS COPIES AND WILL BE PERFORMED BY MORE THAN 2000 ARTISTS...

THE BEATLES CHANGE THE FACE OF ROCK. THEY INTRODUCE NEW SOUNDS AND NEW INSTRUMENTS... ...

...AND THEY WIDEN THE CULTURAL REFERENCES OF ROCK ! . FOR INSTANCE, ON THE SLEEVE OF "SERGEANT PEPPER"...

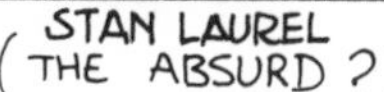

STAN LAUREL (THE ABSURD ?)

MARLÈNE DIETRICH (THE DECADENT ?)

ALBERT EINSTEIN (THE GENIUS ?)

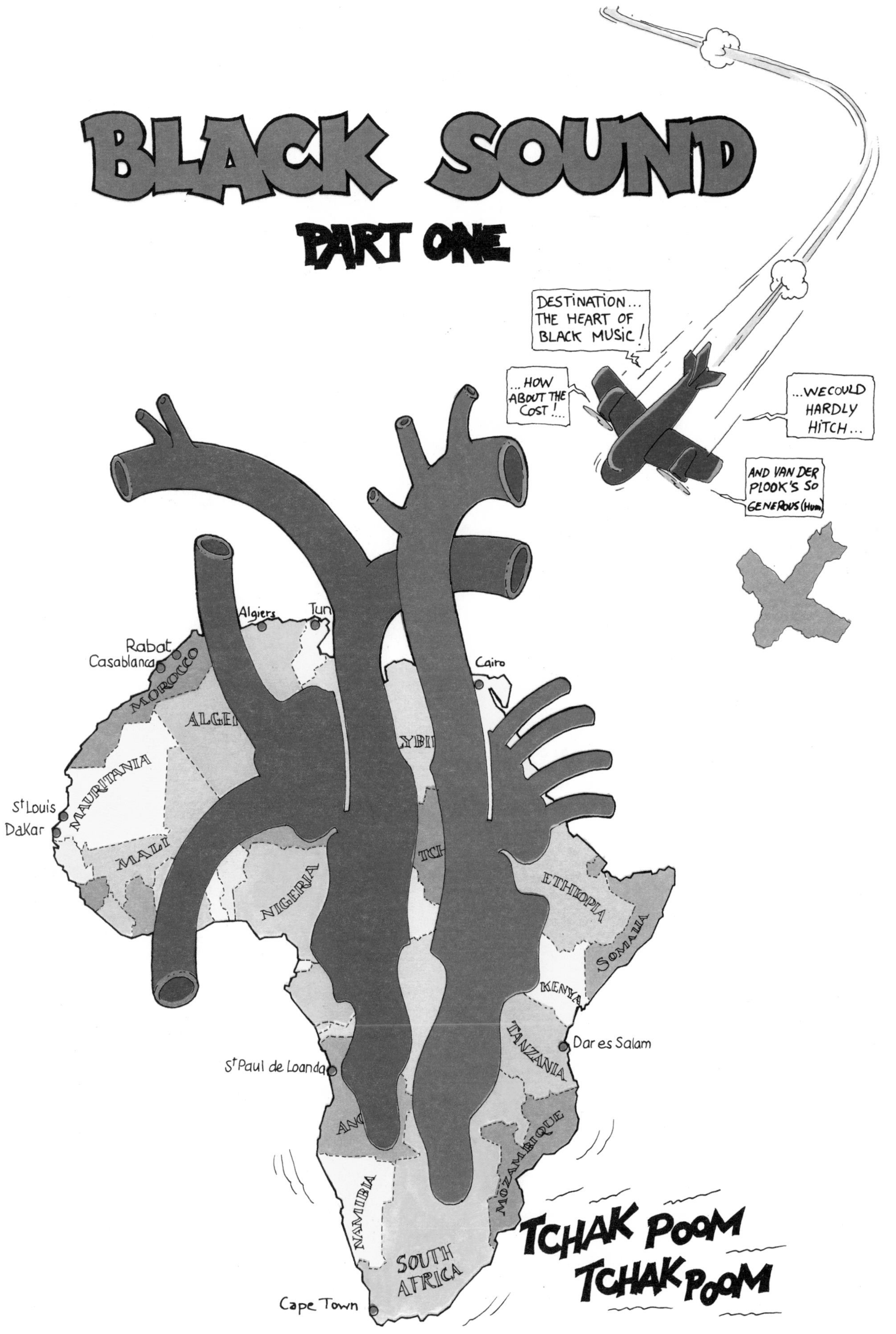

BLACK SOUND
PART ONE
DESTINATION... THE HEART OF BLACK MUSIC!
...HOW ABOUT THE COST!...
...WE COULD HARDLY HITCH...
AND VAN DER PLOOK'S SO GENEROUS (Hum)
Algiers
Rabat
Casablanca
Cairo
MOROCCO
MAURITANIA
St Louis
Dakar
MALI
NIGERIA
ETHIOPIA
SOMALIA
KENYA
TANZANIA
Dar es Salam
St Paul de Loanda
MOZAMBIQUE
NAMIBIA
SOUTH AFRICA
Cape Town
TCHAK POOM
TCHAK POOM

WHAT IS THE BLACK SOUND ?... IN THE DAYS OF SLAVERY...
LIBERTY
... A CRY !...

... IN THE DAYS OF URBAN POVERTY...
... A MEANS OF ESCAPE !...

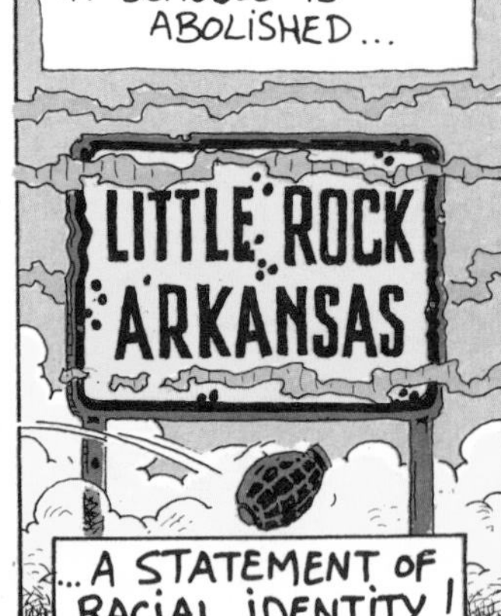

AND AFTER 1954, WHEN SEGREGATION IN SCHOOLS IS ABOLISHED...
LITTLE ROCK ARKANSAS
... A STATEMENT OF RACIAL IDENTITY !

AND THAT'S SOUL FRIENDS ! THE MUSIC THE WHITES CAN'T PLAY !!...
I'VE TRIED... NO WAY !

ALLELUJAH!
SISTERS ! BROTHERS ! WE'RE GOING TO MAKE OUR MUSIC HEARD...
BROTHER RAY CHARLES
BROTHER SAM COOKE
HIPS!
BROTHER JACK DANIELS
ONE SUNDAY MORNING IN THE EARLY '60s, THE WHOLE OF THE FIRST GENERATION OF SOUL IS IN CHURCH ......
LAST NIGHT
WHEN A MAN
OH! NO NOT MY BABY
BOOKER T. JONES
MAXINE BROWN
SWEET SOUL MUSIC
CRY TO ME
PERCY SLEDGE
ARTHUR CONLEY
SOLOMON BURKE
SOUL
LUCILLE
B.B. KING
MUDDY WATERS
JOHN LEE HOOKER
MERCY MERCY ME
JAMES BROWN
WILSON PICKETT
MARVIN GAYE
YAKETY YAK
KING CURTIS
OTIS REDDING
ARETHA FRANKLIN
JOE TEX
SMOKEY ROBINSON
YUM YUM YUM

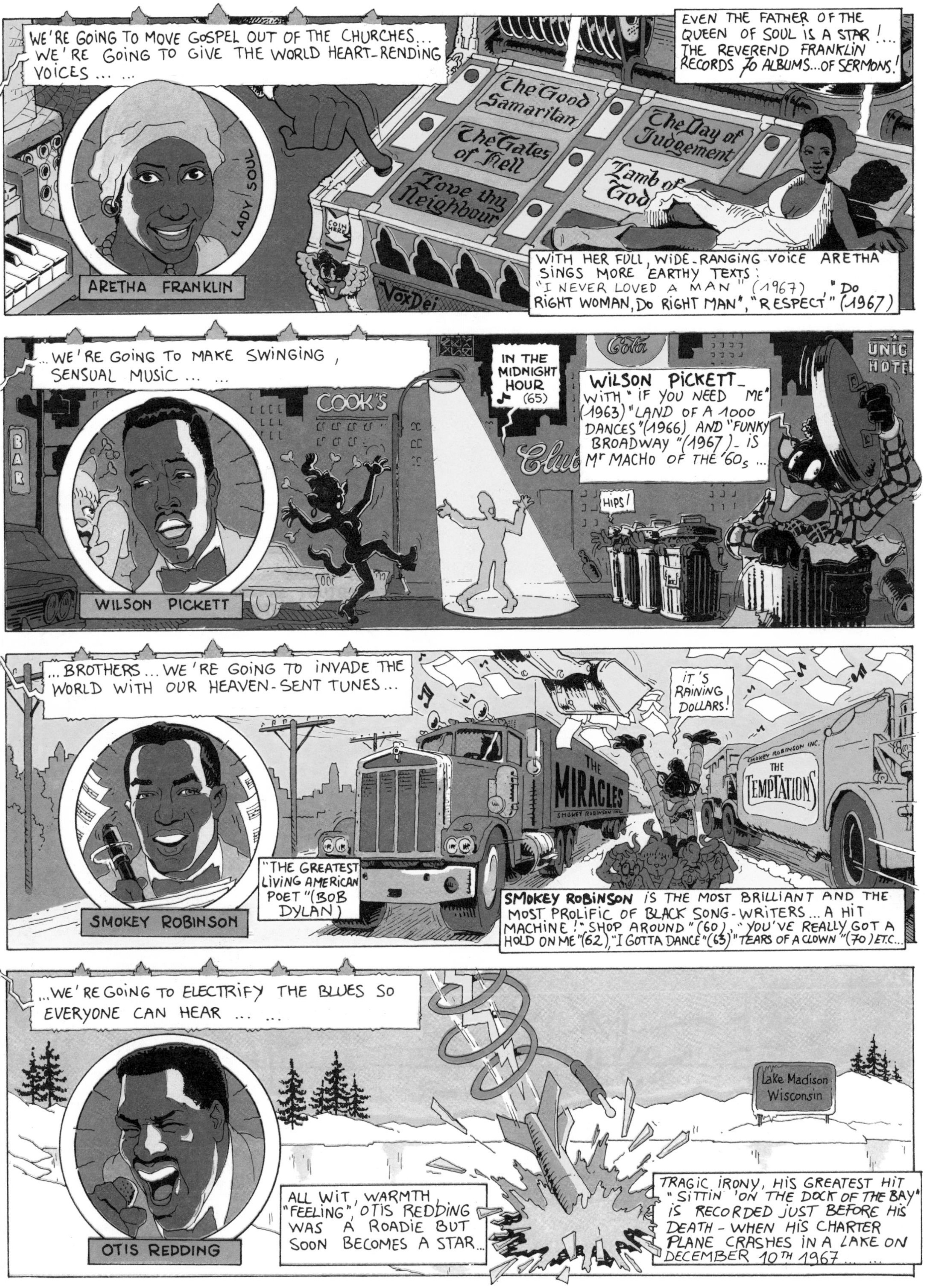

...WE'RE GOING TO ELECTRIFY THE BLUES SO EVERYONE CAN HEAR ... ...

Lake Madison Wisconsin

ALL WIT, WARMTH, "FEELING", OTIS REDDING WAS A ROADIE BUT SOON BECOMES A STAR...

OTIS REDDING

TRAGIC IRONY, HIS GREATEST HIT "SITTIN' ON THE DOCK OF THE BAY" IS RECORDED JUST BEFORE HIS DEATH - WHEN HIS CHARTER PLANE CRASHES IN A LAKE ON DECEMBER 10TH 1967 ... ...

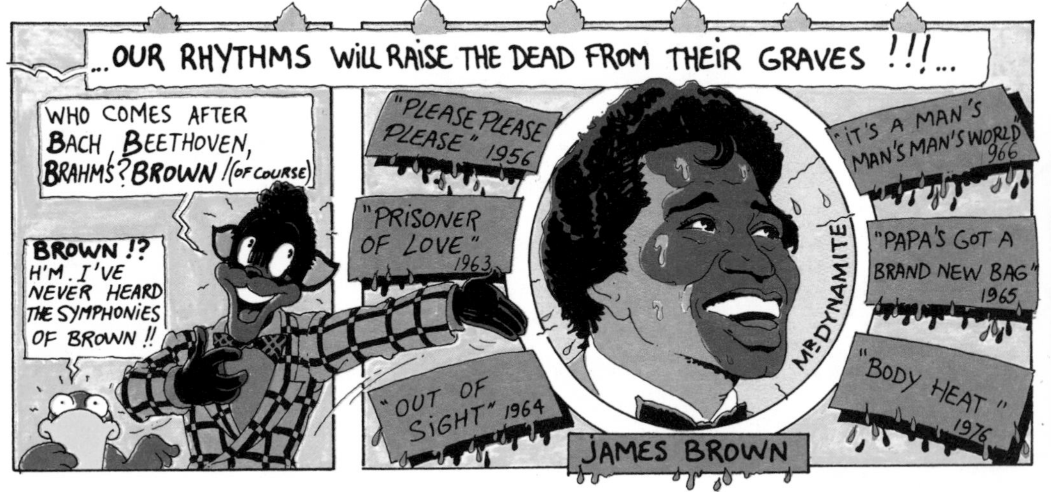
...OUR RHYTHMS WILL RAISE THE DEAD FROM THEIR GRAVES !!!...
WHO COMES AFTER BACH, BEETHOVEN, BRAHMS? BROWN! (OF COURSE)
BROWN!? H'M. I'VE NEVER HEARD THE SYMPHONIES OF BROWN!!
"PLEASE PLEASE PLEASE" 1956
"PRISONER OF LOVE" 1963
"OUT OF SIGHT" 1964
"IT'S A MAN'S MAN'S MAN'S WORLD" 1966
"PAPA'S GOT A BRAND NEW BAG" 1965
"BODY HEAT" 1976
MR DYNAMITE
JAMES BROWN

JAMES BROWN... BORN INTO POVERTY, WORKS AS A SHOE-SHINE BOY, AND AS A BOXER...
THANKS NEGRO
...WORKS HARD!

...EVEN ON STAGE HE NEVER STOPS WORKING... JUST LISTEN TO HIS LEGENDARY "LIVE AT THE APOLLO" ALBUM (65)

"TRY ME" (1958)
1L
CHATEAU BOULOT BROWN 1L
1L
...HE LOSES 6 PINTS* OF SWEAT EACH CONCERT...

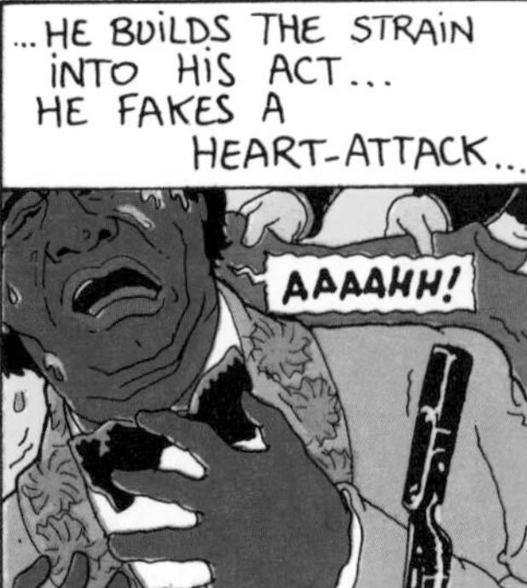
...HE BUILDS THE STRAIN INTO HIS ACT... HE FAKES A HEART-ATTACK...
AAAAHH!

...IS TAKEN TO THE WINGS, A CAPE OVER HIS SHOULDERS, ...

...THEN THROWS OFF THE CAPE AND COMES BOUNDING BACK! BROWN IS RISEN FROM THE DEAD!!
HUM... NEAT IDEA...
MICK JAGGER

JAMES EVEN JUMPS INTO POLITICS, FIGHTING VIOLENCE AND MORAL LAXITY... FROM HARLEM TO VIETNAM... ...

SAY IT LOUD: I'M BLACK AND I'M PROUD...

...AND THEN, SO THE WORLD CAN HEAR OUR MUSIC, WE'RE GOING TO BUILD CORPORATIONS, RICH AND... BLACK!

HIPS!

WE'LL BE BLACK BACK ...NO... HANG ON...

PHEW! I'M GETTING ROCK LAG!!

BERRY GORDY

FORD

DETROIT
MOTOR TOWN
MOTOWN!

SEE YOU SOON, CATS!

ATLANTIC RECORDS is FOUNDED (IT MUST BE ADMITTED) BY TWO TURKS! (WHO BORROW THE MONEY FROM THEIR DENTIST...)

... BUT TAMLA is GUARANTEED 100% PURE BLACK!

* A QUART AND A HALF!!

THE STONES GENERATION
DISGUSTING!
?!
A DISGRACE!
BUT WHAT IS IT !?...
THAT MR BIRD ?! THAT'S MICK THE LICK, THE WHITE ROCKER... WITH THE BLACK SOUND!
CALL THE POLICE AT ONCE DARLING
SEND IT HOME
SHUT YOUR MOUTH!
SHOCKING!
NOT IN FRONT OF THE CHILDREN!
IT'S SCANDALOUS!

THE BRITISH BLUES ARE A RESULT OF THE BRITISH WAY OF LIFE ...
FOR CENTURIES, THE BRITISH HAVE 'LED A SISYPHIAN * EXISTENCE', CAUGHT IN A SOCIO-ECONOMIC TRAP ...
* IN THE GREEK LEGEND, SISYPHUS IS CONDEMNED TO PUSH A ROCK TO THE TOP OF A HILL ... FOREVER !! A SYMBOL OF FUTILITY.
BRITISH BLUES
EDUCATION
POVERTY
SOCIAL CLASS
... A (HOT) SEED BED OF "WORKING CLASS HEROES" ...

THE FATHER OF "THE BLUE-EYED BLUES" ...
THAT'S ME!
FOLKS ...
ALEXIS KORNER OF "BLUES INC."

... INFLUENCES A WHOLE GENERATION OF BRITISH BLUES ROCKERS ... ...
JACK BRUCE OF "CREAM"

ROBERT PLANT OF "LED ZEPPELIN"

... AND ABOVE ALL ... THE MEGA GROUP (THE ROCKIEST ROCKERS IN THE HISTORY OF ROCK)
ROCK (PHEW) SISYPHUS ... R.OCK
COOL ANDRE
... ITS NAME IS A TRIBUTE TO ...

TO WHOM PRAY?
?
?!
TO MUDDY WATERS, STONEBRAIN

"ROLL ...
MICK JAGGER (VOCAL)

... ING ...
KEITH RICHARD (GUITAR)

.. ST ...
BRIAN JONES (GUITAR)

... ONE ...
BILL WYMAN (ELECTRIC BASS)

.. BLUES!"
CHARLIE WATTS (DRUMS)

..FORTUNATELY WE HAVE AMONGST US AN EMINENT STONEOLOGIST! ME ...
RRUH RRUHM
STONELOGY
5 LADS, SONS OF A GYM MASTER, A PIANO TEACHER, A CONSTRUCTION WORKER, AN ELECTRICIAN AND A BUS CONDUCTOR ... ARE GOING TO BLITZ BLIGHTY
(HOW WITTY)
?
CRAP ..!?
PARENTS FIND THE BEATLES NICE AND ACCEPTABLE ...
BUT THE STONES TERRIFY THEM !!! ...
HOW SWEET!
AAAAAAH
GRRRRR..
THEIR FIRST MANAGER ANDREW OLDHAM KEEPS THEM AT THE VERY LIMITS OF SAVAGERY ...
TSK TSK
GGGR
..THEY ARE THE SPEARHEAD OF THE NEW PERMISSIVE SOCIETY ...
YOU'RE TUNED TO RADIO CAROLINE
WHO IS THIS GUY?
TALKS TOO MUCH...
...THE PIRATE RADIO...
City of Westminster
CARNABY S
!!
... IS SHOWING!
MARY! YOUR SLIP...
... MARY QUANT...
I CAN SEE THE MOON!
HEY! WOULD YOU LET YOUR KID SISTER GO OUT WITH A ROLLING STONE
... MINI-SKIRTS ...
WHAOOH!!
LEND ME THE GLASSES!
(SOUND OF A DIRTY MIND)
..THE MODS ...
...AND THE ROCKERS ...
... IN '64, THEIR FIRST ALBUM...
BUT...
DON'T SHOVE...
THE SUCCESS AND THE TOURING BEGIN ...
A KNOCK-OUT THIS ALBUM!
'HOW WITTY'
THE ROLLING STONES
BUT SUCCESS BRINGS PROBLEMS.. THEY ARE ARRESTED FOR URINATING AGAINST A PETROL PUMP..
US!...
IN PUBLIC!
SATISFACTION
AUGUST 20TH 1965 "SATISFACTION" THE HIT WHICH IS FOR THE 60s WHAT "BLUE SUEDE SHOES" WAS FOR THE 50s ...
I'VE HAD ENOUGH!
COME QUICKLY PLEASE OFFICER! THE STONES ARE DESTROYING MY PAGE
APRIL '66 ... "AFTERMATH" - THEIR FIRST CONCEPT ALBUM...
WERE...
THE FIRST TO CONCEIVE!
AFTERMATH
DECCA
JANUARY 13TH 1967 ... THE ONE AND ONLY STONE COMPROMISE ... FOR THE "ED. SULLIVAN SHOW" ... IN THE U.S.A.
WHERE ARE THEY?
"LET'S SPEND THE NIGHT TOGETHER" BECOMES...
BUT... HE LOOKS ANGELIC!
"LET'S SPEND SOME TIME TOGETHER"...
SOMEWHAT NICER SO TO SPEAK...
JULY '67 - FIRST NERVOUS BREAKDOWN OF BRIAN JONES.
HUMPF!
H'M... I CAN SMELL BURNING...
BRIAN JONES
DECEMBER '68 - THE CUSTARD PIE LAUNCHING OF...
Beggars Banquet
MICK TAYLOR REPLACES BRIAN JONES ... JUNE 13TH 1969 ...
Mick Taylor
BRIAN JONES
ARREST THEM!
JANUARY 1971 - THE STONES QUIT GREAT BRITAIN ...
ALL THOSE DATES...
ALL THAT HISTORY...
UP YOURS!
STOP!
...THE FIRST TAX EXILES OF ROCK ...

FIRE !!
AS I WAS SAYING...
THE STONES JET SET...
JEAN-LUC GODARD FILMS THE RECORDING OF "SYMPATHY FOR THE DEVIL" FOR...
CLAP
ONE PLUS ONE
SLATE 4 TAKE 1
ANDY WARHOL DESIGNS THE (DARING!) SLEEVE OF "STICKY FINGERS"
WITH A REAL FLY !!
HEY ! IT'S MICK
MARRIAGE OF MICK AND BIANCA – MAY 12TH '71
AT SAINT-TROPEZ !
Bianca Perez Morena di Macias
IN... ER... LET ME SEE... JUNE...
... JUNE...
JUNE '75... RON WOOD REPLACES MICK TAYLOR
RON WOOD
... BUT NEW FACES IN THE GROUP DON'T AFFECT THEIR SUCCESS OR THEIR MUSICAL IDENTITY GUARANTEED BY THE PRESENCE OF
EXILE ON MAIN STREET 1972
GOATS HEAD SOUP 1973
METAMORPHOSIS 1975
BLACK AND BLUE 1976
IT'S ONLY ROCK'N'ROLL 1974
... MICK JAGGER 40 PLUS AND STILL ROCKING...
HE'LL BE BURYING ME NEXT !!
Some Girls 1978
TATTOO YOU 1981
THAT'S HIM
IS IT ?
MICK THE LICK ?
NO !!
AUTOGRAPH ! PLEASE MICK !
... FOR MY KID SISTER !
... AND OUR MUSIC ?
... WHAT ABOUT OUR MUSIC THEN ?...
YOU HAVE A POINT
LISTEN TO ME, BRAINBOX...
I'M ALL EARS MICK...
OUR MUSIC IS...
... DRUGS
... IN THEIR MUSIC AND IN THEIR LIFE... IN FEBRUARY '65 JAGGER AND RICHARD ARE ARRESTED... JAGGER ACCUSED OF POSSESSING "APHETAMINE SULPHATE" AND "METHYL APHETAMINE HYDRO CHLORIDE"
PEP PILLS !!!
... BUT DRUGS LEAD TO TRAGEDY... VICTIM OF HIS ADDICTION, BRIAN JONES, THE POET OF "LADY JANE", IS FOUND DEAD IN HIS SWIMMING POOL ON JULY 3RD / 69...
JUDGES
"Mother's little helper"
"IN ANOTHER LAND"
THE SENTENCE IS TOUGH !... 12 MONTHS FOR RICHARD AND 3 MONTHS FOR JAGGER... BUT BOTH OF THEM WILL BE ACQUITTED, THANKS (IN PART) TO AN EDITORIAL IN THEIR DEFENCE... IN "THE TIMES" !!
AT A REQUIEM CONCERT IN HYDE PARK JAGGER READS SHELLEY'S "ADONAIS" (WRITTEN ON THE DEATH OF KEATS)
I WEEP FOR ADONAIS – HE IS DEAD O WEEP FOR ADONAIS...
THE TIMES
WHO BREAKS A BUTTERFLY ON A WHEEL ?
"2000 LIGHT YEARS FROM HOME"
"SOMETHING HAPPENED TO ME YESTERDAY"
"ALL SOLD OUT"

...I FIND ALL THIS IN SOMEWHAT DUBIOUS TASTE !...
...SEX
WELL I AM A KING BEE, BUZZING AROUND YOUR HIVE WELL I CAN MAKE HONEY BABY LET ME COME INSIDE."
"UNDER MY THUMB"...
"LET'S SPEND THE NIGHT TOGETHER"
" I CAN'T GET NO SATISFACTION"...
...IT GOES WITHOUT SAYING THAT THE STONES RARELY NEGLECT TO FUSE THE SUGGESTIVE AND THE EROTIC IN THEIR LYRICS...
NOW...THAT'S NEAT.
JOHNNY ROTTEN
"BODY MUSIC"
...HAPPY MEMORIES...
THE MICK JAGGER Souvenir ALBUM
...VIOLENCE
THE STONES FABRICATE AN IMAGE HALF-FACT, HALF-FICTION OF BEING A GANG OF TOUGHS... ALWAYS READY FOR A FIGHT...
...FICTION (?!) BECOMES REALITY AT THE ALTAMONT ROCK FESTIVAL CALIFORNIA 1969... ...
ROLLIN
HOOLIGAN!
"LET IT BLEED"!
GRR
"SYMPATHY FOR THE DEVIL"
"...COS SUMMER'S HERE, AND THE TIME IS RIGHT FOR FIGHTING IN THE STREET, BOY" (STREET FIGHTIN' MAN)
POLICING OF THE CONCERT IS COURTESY OF THE HELL'S ANGELS!...WHO, DURING THE PERFORMANCE, KILL A YOUNG BLACK...

...AND ME!
MICK JAGGER IS UNDOUBTEDLY THE BRIGHTEST STAR IN THE ROCK GALAXY...
... THE VERY INCARNATION OF CHARISMA* (IF YOU'LL PERMIT THE PARADOX)...
... A VERITABLE GULLIVE AMONGST US LILLIPUTIA READY TO EXPLAIN (AN TO EXPLOIT) HIS IMAGE...
*CHARISMA: FAVOUR VOUCHSAFED BY GODS ?!...
DICT
STARDOM...
"I'M NOT IMPORTANT. IT WAS JUST AN INVENTION OF JOURNALISTS..."
MONEY
"... WE BOUGHT THESE ENORMOUS HOUSES SOLD BY THE UPPER CLASSES TO THE MIDDLE CLASSES. I SPENT TEN DAYS IN MINE IN THE LAST EIGHT YEARS ..."
ANDROGYNY...
"IF GOD WANTS ME TO BECOME A WOMAN THEN A WOMAN I WILL BECOME"
SEX...
"SOMETIMES AN ORGASM IS BETTER THAN BEING ON STAGE
SOMETIMES BEING ON STAGE IS BETTER THAN AN ORGASM
DRUGS...
"I HAD THE BUTTERFLIES ONCE... I HAD TO GO OUT AND HAVE HALF A PINT OF BEER"
TEMPERAMENT
"WHEN I GO ON THE ROAD, I JUST GO CRAZY. I BECOME A TOTAL MONSTER"
DEDICATION
..." TRAINING? I GO HORSE RIDING, ROWING AND I'VE GOT A KARATE GUY WHO TRAINS ME ..."
PHILOSOPHY
"DOMESTICITY IS DEATH".
CAMUS! SWIFT! BAYEUX! HUM PRETTY CUTE THIS BOOK! ...
VANITY...
" AS LONG AS MY PICTURE IS ON THE FRONT PAGE
... ... I DON'T CARE WHAT THEY SAY ABOUT ME ON PAGE 96... ...
HOBBIES...
"... PEOPLE HAVE A LOT OF DIFFERENT WAYS OF LETTING OUT THEIR INHIBITIONS ... SEX... LIKE THEY SCREW A LOT, OR DESTROY ROOMS ... ONE INDULGES IN ALL THOSE THINGS
PROVOCATION...
"I HATE ROCK!..."
SOCIOLOGY...
"THE POSITION OF ROCK'N'ROLL IN OUR SUB-CULTURE HAS BECOME FAR TOO IMPORTANT. I THINK ROCK'N'ROLL IS ALL FRIVOLITY. IT SHOULD BE ABOUT SATIN SUITS AND WHITE SOCKS...
THE ENORMOUS SUCCESS OF THE BEATLES AND THE STONES AT THE BEGINNING OF THE '60s STARTS THE BRITISH INVASION OF THE STATES

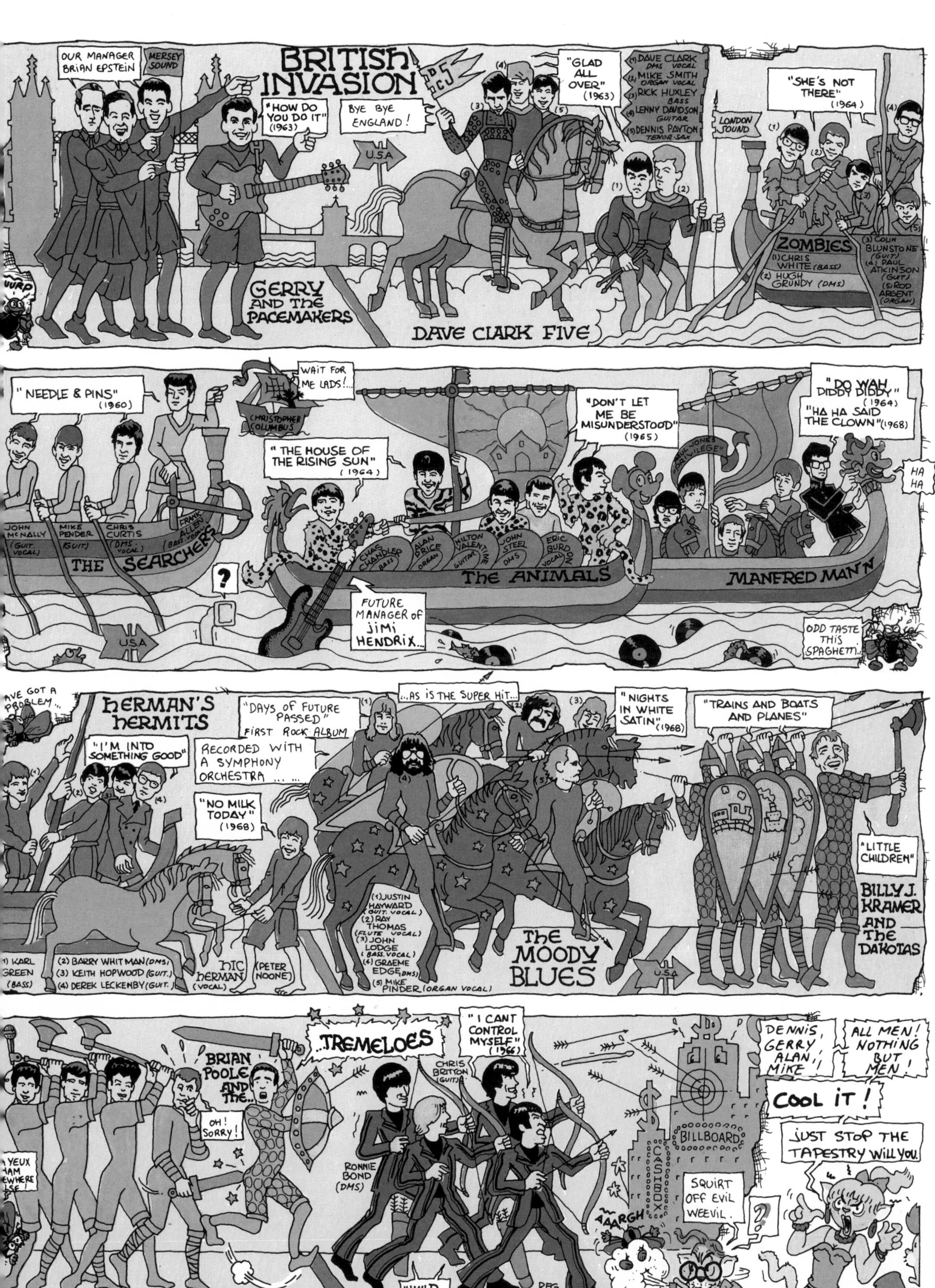
OUR MANAGER BRIAN EPSTEIN
MERSEY SOUND
BRITISH INVASION
"HOW DO YOU DO IT" (1963)
BYE BYE ENGLAND!
U.S.A
"GLAD ALL OVER" (1963)
(1) DAVE CLARK DMS VOCAL
(2) MIKE SMITH ORGAN VOCAL
(3) RICK HUXLEY BASS
(4) LENNY DAVIDSON GUITAR
(5) DENNIS PAYTON TENOR SAX
LONDON SOUND
"SHE'S NOT THERE" (1964)
ZOMBIES
(1) CHRIS WHITE (BASS)
(2) HUGH GRUNDY (DMS)
(3) COLIN BLUNSTONE (GUIT)
(4) PAUL ATKINSON (GUIT)
(5) ROD ARGENT (ORGAN)
GERRY AND THE PACEMAKERS
DAVE CLARK FIVE
"NEEDLE & PINS" (1960)
WAIT FOR ME LADS!...
CHRISTOPHER COLUMBUS
"THE HOUSE OF THE RISING SUN" (1964)
"DON'T LET ME BE MISUNDERSTOOD" (1965)
"DO WAH DIDDY DIDDY" (1964)
"HA HA SAID THE CLOWN" (1968)
HA HA
JOHN McNALLY (GUIT. VOCAL)
MIKE PENDER (GUIT)
CHRIS CURTIS (DMS. VOCAL)
FRANK ALLEN (BASS VOCAL)
THE SEARCHERS
CHAS CHANDLER BASS
ALAN PRICE ORGAN
HILTON VALENTINE GUITAR
JOHN STEEL DMS
ERIC BURDON VOCAL
The ANIMALS
MANFRED MANN
FUTURE MANAGER OF JIMI HENDRIX...
U.S.A
ODD TASTE THIS SPAGHETTI...
HERMAN'S HERMITS
"DAYS OF FUTURE PASSED" FIRST ROCK ALBUM
...AS IS THE SUPER HIT...
"NIGHTS IN WHITE SATIN" (1968)
"TRAINS AND BOATS AND PLANES"
"I'M INTO SOMETHING GOOD"
RECORDED WITH A SYMPHONY ORCHESTRA ... ...
"NO MILK TODAY" (1968)
"LITTLE CHILDREN"
BILLY J. KRAMER AND THE DAKOTAS
(1) JUSTIN HAYWARD (GUIT. VOCAL)
(2) RAY THOMAS (FLUTE VOCAL)
(3) JOHN LODGE (BASS. VOCAL)
(4) GRAEME EDGE (DMS)
(5) MIKE PINDER (ORGAN VOCAL)
THE MOODY BLUES
(1) KARL GREEN (BASS)
(2) BARRY WHITMAN (DMS)
(3) KEITH HOPWOOD (GUIT.)
(4) DEREK LECKENBY (GUIT.)
HIC HERMAN (VOCAL)
(PETER NOONE)
U.S.A
BRIAN POOLE AND THE...
...TREMELOES
"I CANT CONTROL MYSELF" (1966)
CHRIS BRITTON (GUIT)
DENNIS, GERRY, ALAN, MIKE!
ALL MEN! NOTHING BUT MEN!
COOL IT!
JUST STOP THE TAPESTRY WILL YOU.
OH! SORRY!
BILLBOARD
CASHBOX
RONNIE BOND (DMS)
SQUIRT OFF EVIL WEEVIL.
AAARGH
"WILD THING" (1966)
PETER STAPLE (GUIT.)
REG PRESLEY (VOCAL)
The TROGGS
"DA DOO RON RON"
"HERE COMES MY BABY" (1967)

JUST UNBELIEVABLE!..
MEN... MEN... MEN...
WHAT?
THE...

ALL YOU TALK ABOUT IS MEN !!!

WHAT ABOUT WOMEN THEN?
WHERE'S THE PLUG?
AND WHAT ABOUT ME?
WHAT AM I THEN?
PART OF THE FURNITURE?! IS THAT IT?
NICE!

AND WHAT ABOUT HER
WARF
AH! PETULA CLARK!
IS SHE A ROCKER?
BIG HIT WITH "DOWNTOWN" IN '65!
LOOKS LIKE SHE WAS BORN IN AUSTRALIA!

"SUMMER IS OVER"
AND... DUSTY SPRINGFIELD?
GET IT STRAIGHT!

AND DAMN! BLAST!
WANT A HAND SWEETIE?

...AND... CILLA BLACK!
WHO?
NEVER HEARD "LOVE OF THE LOVED?"
IN FACT, HER REAL NAME IS PRISCILLA WHITE!
YES
A LENNON AND Mc-CARTNEY NUMBER!

"THERE IS ALWAYS SOMETHING THERE TO REMIND ME" 1964
QUIET PLEASE
H'M... AND SANDIE SHAW WHO SINGS BAREFOOT...
A SHOE FIRE HIT (OUCH!)

"SHOUT" 1964
AND LULU?
DIG THE HAIR... A GROOVY SCOTS LASS WITH "SOUL"...

"AS TEARS GO BY" - 1964
AND MARIANNE FAITHFULL?...
NOW I REMEMBER HER
MICK JAGGER'S GIRL FRIEND
LUCKY DEVIL!
DID YOU EVER HEAR THE STORY OF HOW SHE AND MICK ...?!!!
RAYMOND!

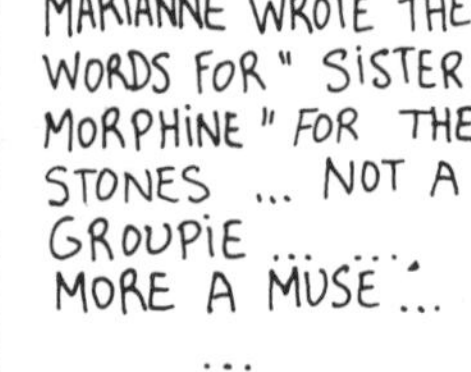
MARIANNE WROTE THE WORDS FOR "SISTER MORPHINE" FOR THE STONES ... NOT A GROUPIE ... MORE A MUSE ...

AS I WAS SAYING, BEFORE I WAS SO RUDELY INTERRUPTED ... WOMEN ROCK STARS EXIST O.K.? SO...
CLIC

...THE NEXT CHAPTER ...
WHO'S GOING TO WRITE IT?
LITTLE ME !! ...
WHAT!!!

BUT COOKIE... I MEAN YOU HAVE TO BE A SPECIALIST...

BUT... I AM A SPECIALIST, AREN'T I CAT?
BUT... ER... I MEAN ... YES OF SORTS... GO AHEAD COOKIE!!

CLEKCLEKCLEK
ARROGANT PIGS...
WE'LL SEE...
I'LL SHOW THEM ANDRE
CLEK
CLEKCLEKCLEK
CLEK

AMERICA IS BEAUTIFUL
TRUE OR FALSE?...
THANKS...
LOVE
PEACE
PFF
ALAN GINSBERG

AMERICA AT THE BEGINNING OF THE '60s ...
...I'M SO NERVOUS.

HOME SWEET HOME
...DEY'S STORE
BUS STOP
HOW'S THINGS?
FINE... JUST FINE.
...A RICH CAREFREE SOCIETY... ...

IN CALIFORNIA, THE 5 BEACH BOYS INVENT...

THE "THEMES"? HOT RODS, SUNSHINE, GIRLS ...

SURF-MUSIC

GOOD VIBRATIONS

"SURFIN U.S.A" (1963)

"THIS CAR OF MINE"

"CATCH A WAVE"

BRIAN WILSON

MIKE LOVE

CARL WILSON

AL JARDINE

DENNIS WILSON

...SUNNY, EASY-GOING, PROFOUNDLY SUPERFICIAL...

...AND THE SUPERB (SIX MONTHS IN RECORDING, A STUDIO BILL OF SOME $ 16,000 !) "GOOD VIBRATIONS" (1966)

BUT THE GILT SOON LEAVES THE GINGERBREAD ...THE CUBAN MISSILE CRISIS (1961)

KRUSHCHEV

...UNDERLINES THE MENACE OF AN ATOMIC WAR ...

BANG!

ON NOVEMBER 22 ND 1963, PRESIDENT JOHN F. KENNEDY IS ASSASSINATED...

THE VIETNAM WAR ESCALATES ... ...

...AND WHO KNOWS WHO'S GOING TO ANSWER THE HOT LINE INSTALLED BETWEEN MOSCOW AND WASHINGTON IN 1963 ... DR STRANGELOVE? (FILM BY STANLEY KUBRICK 1964)

HAHAHA

...THINGS ARE DELICATE... WE'RE WALKING ON EGGS...

...IN SEPTEMBER 1965, BARRY McGUIRE IS No 1 IN THE U.S.A. WITH ...
"EVE OF DESTRUCTION"
BANK
FALL-OUT SHELTER
BLACK PANTHERS
...HOW'S THINGS?
FINE... JUST FINE.
GRRR
GRRR
"THE TIMES THEY ARE A-CHANGIN'"... AS DYLAN SINGS ...

...CHANGE OF MOOD REFLECTED IN THE BEACH BOYS THEMSELVES... ...

BRIAN WILSON
IN 1972
HOLLAND
GET INVOLVED!
...WHO SING A ROCK OF COMMITMENT!

... ALONGSIDE SURF ...
FOLK MUSIC
... A MUSIC WHICH THINKS ...
PFFF
THE GRANDDADDY OF FOLK - WOODY GUTHRIE (WHO DIES IN 1967) SPECIALISES IN TALKING BLUES WHICH TELL OF DRUDGERY, EXPLOITATION AND STRUGGLE ... ...
"A SAINT" SAYS BOB DYLAN
"BOUND FOR GLORY"
HOOTENANNY WITH PETE SEEGER
"GUANTANAMERA"
FOLK MUSIC CIE INCORPORATED
COUNTRY BLUES
URBAN BLUES
... LIKE PETE SEEGER ANOTHER PIONEER OF FOLK, THEY PLAY AT "HOOTENANNIES" THEIR MUSIC GIVES VOICE TO INARTICULATE WORRY/REVOLT ...
IN THE '60s, FOLK PROTESTS AGAINST ALL KINDS OF INJUSTICE ...
EQUAL RIGHTS FOR BLACKS!
FOR ECOLOGY!
AGAINST THE VIETNAM WAR!
FOLK BAR
... PETER, PAUL AND MARY "IF I HAD A HAMMER" "THIS LAND IS YOUR LAND" -
WOODIE GUTHRIE
PETE SEEGER
BOB DYLAN
BORIS VIAN
FOLK ROCK
THE SATIRICAL TOM PAXTON - ARDENT PACIFIST ...
"PEACE WILL COME"
INCREDIBLE STRING BAND
FOLK GUITAR
DONOVAN, THE TROUBADOUR OF BRITISH FOLK " MELLOW YELLOW " (1967)
"SUNSHINE SUPERMAN" 1966
KEROUAC'S ON THE ROAD
I'M A BEATNIK
"SONGS OF LOVE
SIGH
... AND HATE" (1971)
THE MELANCHOLY SOLITARY SENSUAL POET LEONARD COHEN "SUZANNE" 1966
COOKIE, YOU'RE WRITING THIS PAGE REMEMBER
VIET NAM NO
NO
YES
PROTEST MARCH
AND THE WOMEN ... (AND WHAT WOMEN!) THE HIGH PRIESTESSES OF FOLK ...
HIPPY FAMILY
SOUVENIRS
PROTEST SIT-IN
JUDY COLLINS "BOTH SIDES NOW" WHOSE MUSIC TAKES IN FOLK FROM ALL COUNTRIES ...
JUDITH
"WE SHALL OVERCOME"
"UNIVERSAL SOLDIER"
"WHAT HAVE THEY DONE TO THE RAIN"
BAN THE BOMB
LOVE
AND THE PASSIONARIA, THE MADONNA OF FOLK MUSIC OF THE '60s JOAN BAEZ ... WHO DREAMS OF CHANGING THE WORLD WITH A SONG.
"DON'T THINK TWICE IT'S ALL RIGHT"
A WHOLE ARMY OF RADICAL SINGERS LINK ARMS BEHIND A CERTAIN ROBERT ZIMMERMAN ...

...BUT WHO IS

"THAT IS THE QUESTION"!

...THE CHILD WHO QUITS HOME LIKE RIMBAUD?...

...THE FRAGILE ADOLESCENT WHO CHANGES HIS NAME AS A TRIBUTE TO THE WELSH POET DYLAN THOMAS?...

...THE REBEL WHO LEADS THE LIFE OF A BUM "ON THE ROAD" LIKE A KEROUAC HERO?

...THE POLITICAL ARTIST WHO, FROM GREENWICH VILLAGE TO BERKELEY, SINGS PROTEST SONGS?

"A HARD RAIN'S GONNA FALL"
"MASTERS OF WAR"

BLOWIN' IN THE WIND

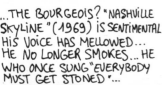

...SUNG BY AN AUDIENCE OF 35,000 AT HIS TRIUMPHANT NEWPORT APPEARANCE ALONGSIDE JOAN BAEZ IN '63...

...THE PROPHET OF A RESPONSIBLE GENERATION, WHICH TRANSFORMS MINDLESS ROCK INTO THINKING ROCK?...
"THE TIMES THEY ARE A-CHANGIN'"!...

...THE ICONOCLAST WHO WITH THE ALBUM "BRINGING IT ALL BACK HOME" (1965) "ELECTRIFIES" FOLK?...

!SACRILEGE!

AN AMPLIFIED GUITAR!

!BLASPHEMY

COMMERCIALISM

GRRR GRRR

GRRR!!

.... PAVING THE WAY FOR THE MAGNIFICENT "BLONDE ON BLONDE" (1966)

...THE RECLUSE?... SILENT FOR TWO YEARS AFTER A SERIOUS MOTOR CYCLE ACCIDENT IN '66...

THE OBTUSE? THE SIMPLE COUNTRY STYLE OF "JOHN WESLEY HARDING"... ...

...WHEN EVERYONE ELSE HAS GONE PSYCHEDELIC.

...THE BOURGEOIS? "NASHVILLE SKYLINE" (1969) IS SENTIMENTAL HIS VOICE HAS MELLOWED... HE NO LONGER SMOKES... HE WHO ONCE SUNG "EVERYBODY MUST GET STONED"...

DON'T LOOK BOURGEOIS TO ME!

EVEN SINGING ALONGSIDE JOHNNY CASH ON T.V. (RIMBAUD WANTS TO BE ELVIS?!)...

... THE ACTOR-PRODUCER IN THE MOVIES...

Renaldo & Clara

...THE BORN AGAIN CHRISTIAN ON THE ALBUM "SLOW TRAIN COMING"...

...THE DISENCHANTED? "SAVED" (1980) AND "INFIDELS" (1984)...

...AND SO IT GOES ON...
WHICH ONE IS BOB DYLAN?
...DYLAN IS ALL OF THEM!
MULTIPLE...
PROTEAN...
COMPLEX...
ENIGMATIC

BUT... WITH A SECRET INGREDIENT

GENIUS!

...AFTER SURF AND FOLK ...
FOLK-ROCK ...
THINGS ARE GETTING COMPLICATED
... FOLK-ROCK STEMS FROM THE BEATLES AND FROM THE ELECTRIC DYLAN ...
THE LYRICS ARE "MEANINGFUL" (FOLK STYLE) ...
... BUT CLOTHED IN ELABORATE MUSICAL DISGUISES, CONCOCTED IN THE STUDIO-LABORATORIES BY THE GREAT MUSICAL FIXERS ... - GEORGE MARTIN (OF BEATLES FAME) AND...
... THE FAMOUS PHIL ... SPECTOR'S SPECTRE STILL HAUNTS ROCK !
CRYSTALS - DARLENE LOVE
BOB B. SOX AND THE BLUE JEANS
RIGHTEOUS BROTHERS - RONETTES
JOHN PHILLIPS
DENNY DOHERTY
MICHELLE GILLIAM
CASS ELLIOTT
"DEDICATED TO THE ONE I LOVE" 1967
...ON THE EAST COAST JOHN SEBASTIAN'S LOVIN' SPOONFUL MAKES ITS MARK WITH "DAYDREAM" (APRIL '66) AND THE BRILLIANT "SUMMER IN THE CITY" (N°1 IN JULY '66)
... ON THE WEST COAST THE MAMAS AND THE PAPAS REPEL THE BRITISH INVADER WITH THEIR CLASSY HIPPY STYLE AND THEIR FABULOUS "SOUND"... "CALIFORNIA DREAMIN" (1966) "MONDAY MONDAY" (1967)
...NON-CONFORMIST... AND MARRIED ! SONNY AND CHER (PREVIOUSLY KNOWN AS CEASAR AND CLEO AND THEN NAPOLEON AND JOSEPHINE) SING OF NUPTIAL BLISS AND OTHER VICES ...
"I GOT YOU BABE" 1965 "BANG BANG" 1966 "THE BEAT GOES ON"
WHAT A BUSINESS !
... MORE CHIC ... THE TURTLES - "IT AIN'T ME BABE" THEIR FIRST HIT COMPOSED BY DYLAN IN '65, "HAPPY TOGETHER" IN 1967...
PAUL
GEORGE
JOHN
RINGO
... THE STUDIOS EVEN SPAWN AN IMITATION OF THE BEATLES - THE TELEGENIC BUT MUSICALLY INCOMPETENT MONKEES RECRUITED VIA THE CLASSIFIED ADS ... THEIR OVERNIGHT SUCCESS MEANS THEY HAVE TO LEARN TO PLAY THE GUITAR ... FAST !...
DAVY JONES
MIKE NESMITH
MICKY DOLENZ
PETER TORK
HANG ON COOKIE ! JUST A MO' ... !
BYRDS
SCENE XII
ANDRE/COOKIE
A: WHAT ABOUT BUFFALO SPRINGFIELD ?... AND THE CARPENTERS ? AND LAURA NYRO ? AND
C: NOT ROOM FOR EVERYONE !
A: ...AND THE BYRDS ?!
C: I'M GETTING THERE ! (SHE SIGHS)
A: BUT JUST LOOK WHAT'S LEFT OF THE PAGE : 3 FRAMES !!!
C: COOL IT ANDRE !
A: LOOK COOKIE, THIS IS THE GENEALOGICAL TREE OF THE BYRDS ! IT'S 3 YARDS LONG
C: IS THAT REALLY ESSENTIAL HONEY ?
A: PRECISELY WHAT IS ESSENTIAL ?
C: WAIT AND SEE, ANDRE BABY. WAIT AND SEE...
FOLK-ROCK AT ITS GREATEST ... THE BYRDS UNDER THE DIRECTION OF ROGER McGUINN...
FOLK-ROCK...
THEY'RE TAKING THE MYCKY !
BYRDS
... HAVE A BIG BIG HIT IN '65 WITH DYLAN'S: "Mr TAMBOURINE MAN"...
THE BYRDS DONT STOP AT FOLK-ROCK ... THEY EXPLORE COSMIC ROCK WITH: "FIFTH DIMENSION" ('66)
...SPACE-ROCK...
THE MUSIC OF THE SPHERES
BLUEGRASS...
OR COUNTRY ?
... AND COME BACK DOWN TO EARTH WITH THE COUNTRY "SWEETHEART OF THE RODEO"... (1968)

LAST FACET OF THE PERIOD '62 - '68... A COUSIN OF FOLK-ROCK...
FOLK
FOLK ROCK
CAMPUS ROCK
...CAMPUS-ROCK - A ROCK CLOSE TO THE LIFE AND TIMES OF STUDENTS.
THAT'S ME!

AT A NEW YORK HIGH SCHOOL TWO FRIENDS ACT IN "ALICE IN WONDERLAND"
HEY ALICE!
...THE SMALL ONE - THE WHITE RABBIT... AND THE TALL ONE - THE CHESHIRE CAT...

IN 1956, THE TWO FRIENDS SING ON THE DICK CLARK T.V. SHOW...
"HEY SCHOOLGIRL"
THEY CALL THEMSELVES "TOM & JERRY".

IT'S NOT UNTIL '64, THANKS TO THE PRODUCER TOM WILSON - RESPONSIBLE FOR THE "ELECTRIFICATION" OF DYLAN
"THE SOUNDS OF SILENCE"
...THAT THE TWOSOME BECOM
SIMON AND GARFUNKEL

"AMERICA"
...(PRE-SPRINGSTEEN)... PATRIOTISM...

...WITH ELEGANCE, PURITY AND HINT OF SUGAR, THEY SING OF EVERYDAY HANG-UPS... ...
EEECH

...OLD AGE: "OLD FRIENDS" FROM THE ALBUM BOOKENDS.

"PARANOÏA BLUES"
AVERAGE PERPLEXED STUDENT
STOP
...PEACE OF MIND... "A BRIDGE OVER TROUBLED WATERS" IN 1970... (2 MILLIONS COPIES SOLD IN 3 WEEKS)...
... A "SOFT(?)-ROC

...SEXUALITY... "MRS ROBINSON"... THE MUSIC FROM THE MIKE NICHOLS' FILM "THE GRADUATE" (1967)...
HEY! MRS ROBINSON!
HELP DUSTIN!
GULP

KRR
"GOOD OLD BOYS"
...LESS SATIRICAL, MORE MIDDLE-CLASS THAN THE HARDER-HITTING ROCK OF RANDY NEWMAN AND HARRY NILSSON...

EUREKA !!...
THE CHAPTER'S FINISHED ...
BRAVO COOKIE!...
OH! ♡ ♡ CAT...
EVEN A BUNCH OF DAISIES FROM VAN DER PLOOK!
HOW LAVISH!
HUMPH! PFF!!
SMACK

...AND WHO ARE YOU GOING TO ASK TO WRITE THE NEXT CHAPTER?...
...THE CLEANING LADY?...

NO CATS!...
... ME!
BLACK IS BACK!!
WITH AN INVITATION
CLIC
?!!
!

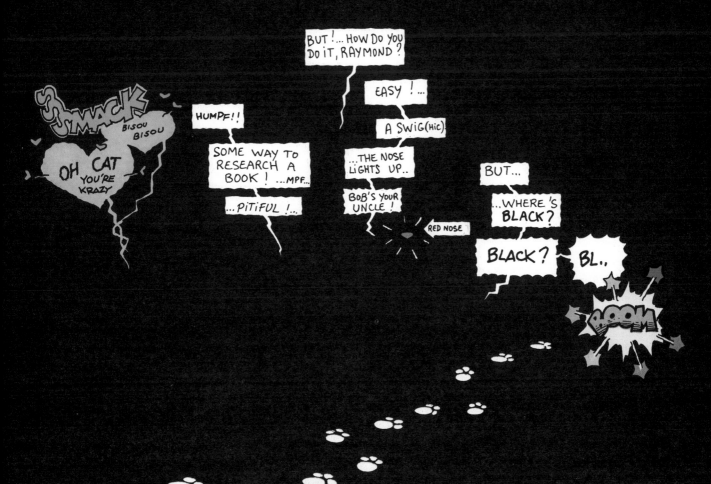

SMACK
BISOU BISOU
OH CAT YOU'RE KRAZY
HUMPF!!
SOME WAY TO RESEARCH A BOOK! ...MPF...
...PITIFUL!...
BUT!... HOW DO YOU DO IT, RAYMOND?
EASY!...
A SWIG (HIC)
...THE NOSE LIGHTS UP..
BOB'S YOUR UNCLE!
RED NOSE
BUT...
...WHERE'S BLACK?
BLACK?
BL..
BOOM

APOLLO
TICKETS FOR THE THEATRE!
FOR THE APOLLO IN HARLEM!
FOR A BIG SHOW FEATURING THE CREAM OF BLACK-MUSIC ...

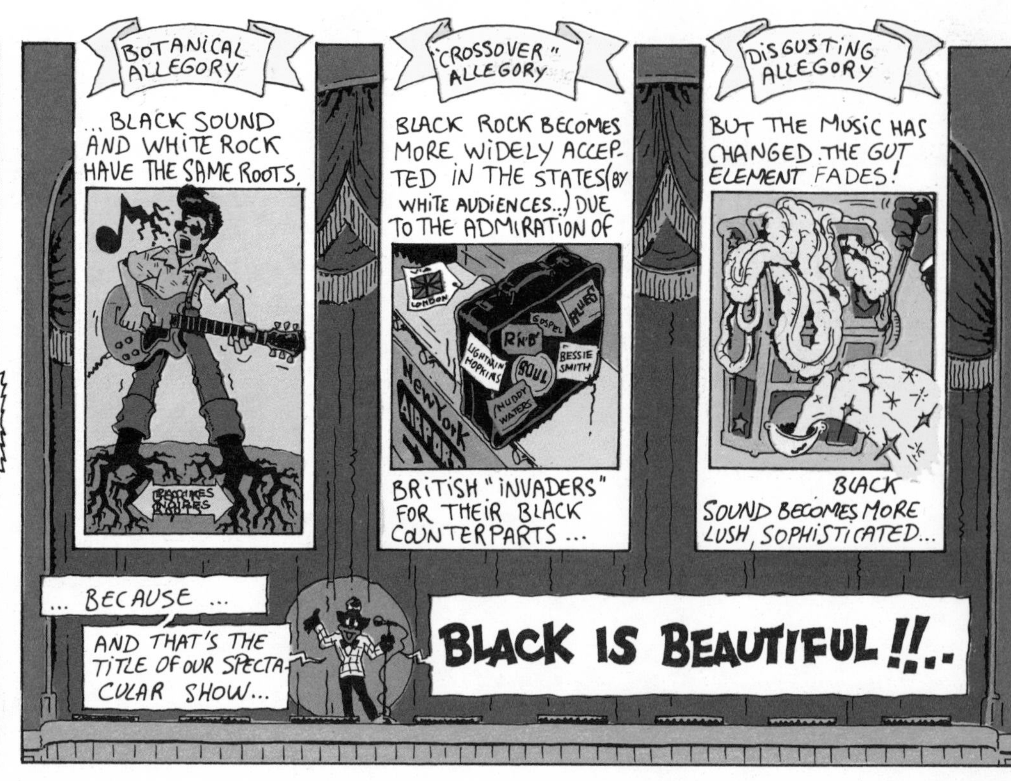
BOTANICAL ALLEGORY
... BLACK SOUND AND WHITE ROCK HAVE THE SAME ROOTS,
"CROSSOVER" ALLEGORY
BLACK ROCK BECOMES MORE WIDELY ACCEPTED IN THE STATES (BY WHITE AUDIENCES...) DUE TO THE ADMIRATION OF
R'n'B
GOSPEL
BLUES
SOUL
BESSIE SMITH
MUDDY WATERS
NEW YORK
BRITISH "INVADERS" FOR THEIR BLACK COUNTERPARTS ...
DISGUSTING ALLEGORY
BUT THE MUSIC HAS CHANGED THE GUT ELEMENT FADES!
BLACK SOUND BECOMES MORE LUSH, SOPHISTICATED...
... BECAUSE ...
AND THAT'S THE TITLE OF OUR SPECTACULAR SHOW...
BLACK IS BEAUTIFUL!!..

THE PRODUCERS OF THE SHOW?...
THE TERRIBLE THREE...
ONLY...THERE'S FOUR OF THEM!
Hitsville USA
BERRY GORDY Jr. WHO QUITS HIS JOB ON THE FORD ASSEMBLY LINE TO LAUNCH MOTOWN
BUT, IT'S YOU Mr GORDY!
AHMET ERTEGUN & JERRY WEXLER OF ATLANTIC.
DRRIING
JIM STEWART OF STAX.

AND NEXT-DOOR...
...THE SONG WRITER'S SWEAT SHOP...
BUT THEY'RE WORKING LIKE...
GLURG
A SONG = A STORY
SMOKEY ROBINSON
NORMAN WHITFIELD
"I HEARD IT THROUGH THE GRAPEVINE" (1968)

IN REHEARSAL ROOM No 1...
THE SUPREMES!
SUBLIME DIANA!
TYPICAL! THEY ONLY HAVE EYES FOR HER!...
"WE DID OUR LOVE GO"
"BABY LOVE"
"STOP IN THE NAME OF LOVE"
"I HEAR A SYMPHONY"
IT TAKES TIME FOR DIANA ROSS AND HER FRIENDS FROM DOWNTOWN DETROIT TO MAKE THE BREAK
BUT WHEN THEY DO, THEY FAST BECOME THE MOST POPULAR VOCAL GROUP OF ALL TIME
INTERNATIONAL TALENT MANAGEMENT INC.
A "SUPREME" GOWN: DETAIL
BEAUTIFUL, LUXURIOUS, CHIC... JUST LIKE THE MUSIC...

...KNOCKING AT THE STAGE DOOR, GLADYS KNIGHT AND THE PIPS...!
STAGE DOOR
WE WANT TO SEE MARVIN GAYE!
HE'S WORKING ON OUR FIRST HIT!

...REHEARSAL ROOM Nº 2 ...
...THE DISCOVERY OF DIANA ROSS ...
THE JACKSON FIVE (RANDY, MICHAEL, JERMAINE, MARLON, TITO & JACKIE)...
"DANCING MACHINE"
I'LL TAKE THAT ONE...
MICHAEL
SCOOP! THE JACKSON FIVE ARE SIX !!
IT'S DAD... HE WANTS SOME POCKET MONEY...
RANDY
THE JACKSON SMILE.
TOOTHPASTE ROCK ?
CHAOS IN THE APOLLO LOBBY ...
ALL THE VOCAL GROUPS HAVE ARRIVED AT THE SAME TIME !
"DANCE TO THE MUSIC" 1967 (SLY AND THE FAMILY STONE)
ARE YOU A FOUR TOP?
NO, I'M A TEMPTATION!
"I CANT HELP MYSELF"!
"REACH OUT I'LL BE THERE" (THE FOUR TOPS) 1966
SAM, WHERE ARE YOU ?
BROTHER BROTHER
"THE WAY YOU DO THE THINGS YOU DO" '69
"PAPA WAS A ROLLING STONE" 1972 (THE TEMPTATIONS)
I'M HERE BROTHER!
SLY? ANYONE SEEN SLY?
"THIS OLD HEART OF MINE" 1966 (THE ISLEY BROTHERS)
"HOLD ON I'M COMIN" (SAM & DAVE) 1966
DAVE WHERE ARE YOU ?!
IN THE DRESSING ROOMS ...
"WALK ONLY"
DON'T DISTURB WHEN MOSES COMPOSES !
OLD MACHO BLACK MOSES !
SIR ISAAC
ISAAC HAYES PENS THE MUSIC FOR THE FILM "SHAFT" (1971)
MR GORDY... DO I HAVE TO SING? ...
PLEASE, MARVIN, JUST FOR ME. PLEASE!
MARVIN GAYE - TORMENTED, NATURE-LOVING, MYSTICAL ...
MARVIN
"WHAT'S GOING ON" IS THE FIRST CONCEPT ALBUM FROM A BLACK ARTIST ...
CURTIS MAYFIELD - THE COMPOSER OF "ROOTS" AND OF "SUPERFLY"...
UM, UM,
ER, ER,
BLACK POWER
CONTRAT
...CAN'T CHOOSE BETWEEN BLACK POWER AND SHOWBIZ ...
IN THE DRESSING-ROOM OF IKE AND TINA TURNER. IT'S A HELL HOUSE !
WHO'S THIS MICK JAGGER ON THE PHONE ?!...
"A FOOL IN LOVE"
"IDOLIZE YOU"
"THE HUNTER"
"PROUD MARY"
"HONKY TONK WOMAN"
SONNY BOY WILLIAMSON
DIES IRAE
NOT SHORT ENOUGH...
WHERE ARE THE CHAINS?
TOO HOT TO HOLD
THE COSTUME OF THE SEX QUEEN OF ROCK: DETAIL
THE "ANTI-ROSS" STYLE ...

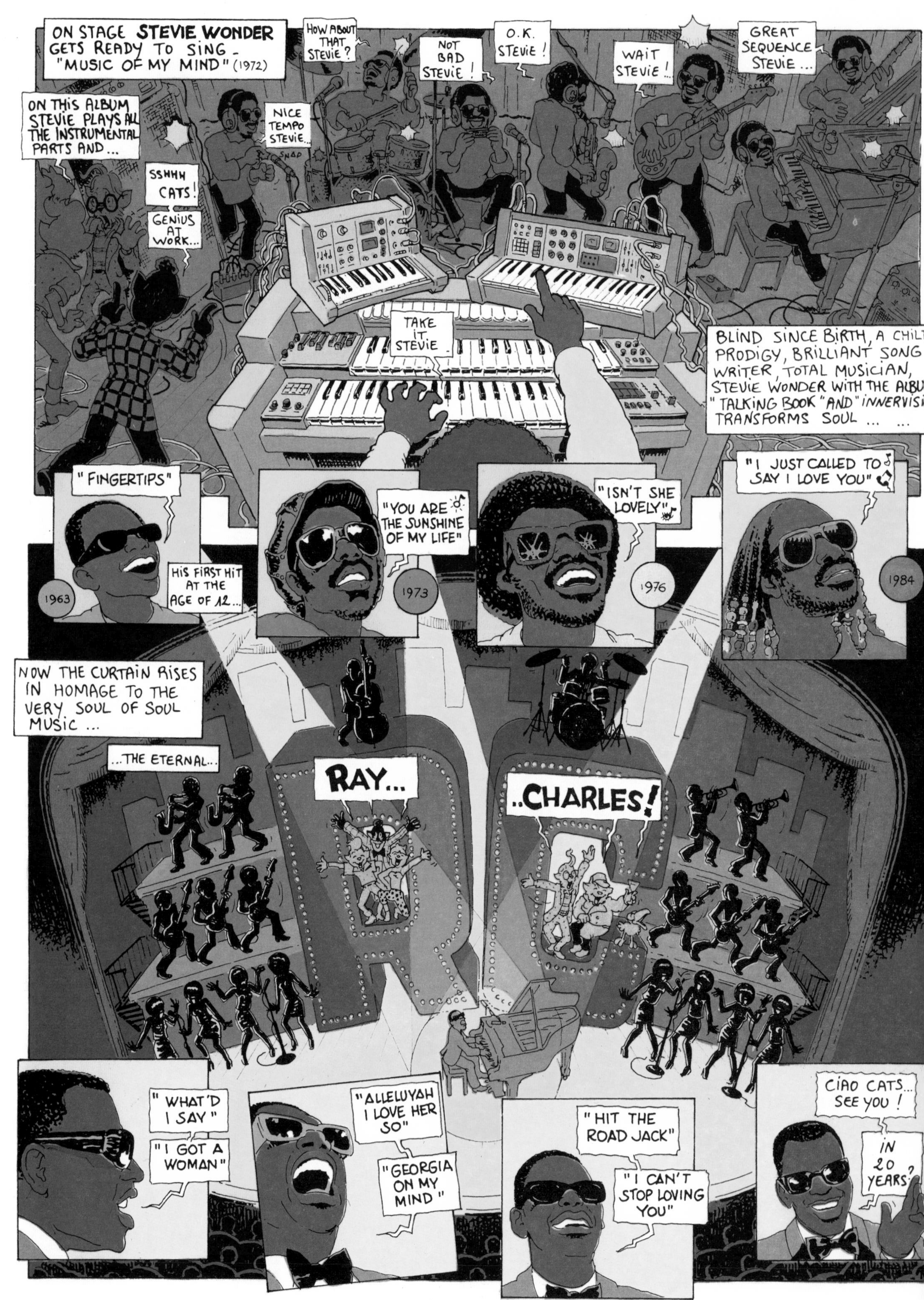
ON STAGE STEVIE WONDER GETS READY TO SING - "MUSIC OF MY MIND" (1972)
HOW ABOUT THAT STEVIE?
NOT BAD STEVIE!
O.K. STEVIE!
WAIT STEVIE!
GREAT SEQUENCE STEVIE...
ON THIS ALBUM STEVIE PLAYS ALL THE INSTRUMENTAL PARTS AND...
NICE TEMPO STEVIE...
SNAP
SSHHH CATS!
GENIUS AT WORK...
TAKE IT STEVIE
BLIND SINCE BIRTH, A CHILD PRODIGY, BRILLIANT SONG WRITER, TOTAL MUSICIAN, STEVIE WONDER WITH THE ALBUMS "TALKING BOOK" AND "INNERVISIONS" TRANSFORMS SOUL ... ...
"FINGERTIPS"
HIS FIRST HIT AT THE AGE OF 12...
1963
"YOU ARE THE SUNSHINE OF MY LIFE"
1973
"ISN'T SHE LOVELY"
1976
"I JUST CALLED TO SAY I LOVE YOU"
1984
NOW THE CURTAIN RISES IN HOMAGE TO THE VERY SOUL OF SOUL MUSIC ...
...THE ETERNAL...
RAY...
..CHARLES!
"WHAT'D I SAY"
"I GOT A WOMAN"
"ALLELUYAH I LOVE HER SO"
"GEORGIA ON MY MIND"
"HIT THE ROAD JACK"
"I CAN'T STOP LOVING YOU"
CIAO CATS... SEE YOU!
IN 20 YEARS?

SUPERGROUPS & GUITAR HEROES
- VAN DER PLOOK LTD -

IN SWINGING LONDON AT THE END OF THE '60s, THERE EMERGES A NEW MOD ROCK ELITE
... BORN OF THE BRITISH BLUES ...
JOHN MAYALL
GEORGIE FAME
FREE
STEVIE WINWOOD
AND ABOVE ALL THE GREAT JOE COCKER
BLUES BUSINESS
SHARE INDEX
"BLUESBREAKERS" 66 "A HARD ROAD" 67 "THE BLUES ALONE"
ex BLUE FLAMES "YEH YEH" 64 "BONNIE & CLYDE" 68
"TON OF SOBS" "FIRE & WATER" "ALL RIGHT NOW" 70
ex SPENCER DAVIS GROUP ex TRAFFIC... "KEEP ON RUNNIN'" 66
"MARJORINE" "NIDNIGHT RIDER"
NEW YORK
LONDON
... AN ANARCHIC ELITE ...
SMASHED: 1 DRUM KIT
SLASHED: 2 UNION JACK SUITS
BURNT: 1 ELECTRIC GUITAR
RIPPED OUT: 4 MICROPHONES
EXPLODED: 3 AMPLIFIERS
LOST: A CERTAIN IMAGE OF ENGLAND
... A BOMB? ...
NO...
JUST A WHO CONCERT!
PETE TOWNSHEND GUITAR
KEITH MOON DRUMS
2 IMPISH NIHILISTS!
JOHN ENTWHISTLE BASS
ROGER DALTREY VOCAL
"MY GENERATION" (1965)
"A QUICK ONE WHILE HE'S AWAY" (1966)
THE ROCK-OPERA TOMMY 1969
... A DECADENT ELITE ...
THE KINKS SING WITH ACID DETACHMENT ...
... OF THE WARPED VALUES OF A CHANGING ENGLAND ... ...
WHAT A BORE!
... THE ENGLISH SUNDAY "SUNNY AFTERNOON" 1966
... CONSERVA-TIVE PROPRIETY "A WELL RESPECTED MAN" 1966 ...
... AND ATROPHY ... IN 1969 THE ROCK-OPERA "ARTHUR OR THE DECLINE AND FALL OF THE BRITISH EMPIRE".
OH DEAR!
ROCK-OPERA ... THE FIRST OF THE GENRE "OGDEN'S NUT GONE" BY THE SMALL FACES & "S.F. SORROW" BY THE PRETTY THINGS.
CLASSY NO?
THE LACONIC AND LEGENDARY RAY DAVIES, WRY LYRICIST ...
... GEAR "DEDICATED FOLLOWER OF FASHION ...
... A PROGRESSIVE ELITE ...
THE AMBITIOUS PROCOL HARUM ...
PROCOL HARUM IS THE NAME OF A CAT! ...
IN LATIN IT MEANS
... AND ITS INSPIRED NEO-BAROQUE UNIVERSAL HIT "A WHITER SHADE OF PALE" (1967) ...
... BASED ON THE ... HUM ... SUITE No 3 IN D. MINOR BY J.S. BACH ...
PROCOL HARUM a whiter shade of pale
WHAT THE HELL ARE YOU GIRLS DOING?
GOT A LIGHT LOVE?
WE'RE THE WORDS (BY KEITH REID) OF "A WHITER SHADE OF PALE"
"16 VESTAL VIRGINS LEAVING FOR THE COAST" ...
I NEED A BLOKE!
FED UP!
SEAGULL KEBAB ... AGAIN ...
PFF
BURP

BUT A SUPER-ELITE IS BORN AMONGST THE VIRTUOSO... STARS OF THE GUITAR

...THE GUITAR HAS EVOLVED SINCE THE '30s !
WARF! WARF!

IN THE OLD DAYS A NOTE PLAYED ON THE GUITAR...
TOOT
TOOT
WAS DROWNED!
TOOT

IN 1939 CHARLIE CHRISTIAN, GUITARIST WITH BENNY GOODMAN...
THANKS CHARLIE.
...INSTALLS A MIKE AND AN AMPLIFIER!...

RESULT: AT LAST YOU CAN HEAR IT! ...
DOING
WHO'S THE UPSTART?

...AND, AMPLIFIED, UNDERGOES A CHANGE OF PERSONALITY!
DOIIINNNGG
ENTER DISTORTION!...

MEANWHILE, BACK AT THE LAB LEO FENDER IS AT WORK... (GIBSON'S RIVAL)...
GREAT STUFF LEO!...
Fender

FIRST HIT BY THE NEW STYLE GUITAR...
WELL DONE, ARTHUR!
GUITAR BOOGIE
BY ARTHUR "FINGERS" SMITH
THE FIRST C AND W HIT TO STRIKE GOLD!...

...THERE FOLLOWS A SERIES OF PAINFUL OPERATIONS... ... ...
FEEDBACK...

THE WAH-WAH PEDAL...

THE SUSTAIN...

IRONY! IN 1978, MARK KNOPFLER OF DIRE STRAITS WILL TRY ELECTRONICALLY... ...
SMART MARK
...TO REDISCOVER THE SOUND OF THE ACOUSTIC GUITAR.

THE MAJORITY OF GUITAR HEROES ARE BRITISH...
PETER GREEN (EX BLUESBREAKERS) OF FLEETWOOD MAC
JEFF BECK
STEVE MARRIOTT OF THE SMALL FACES...
JIMMY PAGE OF THE YARDBIRDS, WHERE HE REPLACES JEFF BECK...
Fender STRATOCASTER
ALVIN LEE OF TEN YEARS AFTER
KEITH RICHARD OF THE ROLLING STONES...
PETE TOWNSHEND OF THE WHO
...AND THE GREATEST, THE FASTEST, THE HERO OF HEROES ...
... KNOWN AFFECTIONATELY AS ...

"GOD"!
...ERIC CLAPTON (EX-YARDBIRDS) WHO TEAMS UP WITH ...
...SUPERSTAR BASSIST JACK BRUCE...
AND SUPERSTAR DRUMMER GINGER BAKER...
...TO FORM THE SUPERSTAR GROUP WITH THE SUPERSTAR (AND IMMODEST)... NAME OF
PLOOT
CREAM
"DISRAELI GEARS" 1967
"WHEELS OF FIRE" 1968
BUT EVEN "GOD" HAS A GOD ... ... PRIMUS INTER PARES, THE IMMORTAL (AND AMERICAN) ... ...
JIMI HENDRIX
"FOXY LADY" 1967
"HEY JOE" 1967
"ARE YOU EXPERIENCED" 1967
"ELECTRIC LADYLAND" 1968
"VOODOO CHILE" 1970
HIS GUITAR... A MACHINE-GUN?
A MAGIC WAND?
...ON STAGE HENDRIX IS THE HIGH PRIEST OF A STRANGE RELIGION ...
...A WOMAN?
...A SONG BIRD?...
HIMMEL!
A... (?)...? (SIGMUND GOES PALE)
LIKE TOWNSHEND OF THE WHO ...
...LIKE EMERSON OF THE NICE, WHO DESTROYS HIS HAMMOND ORGAN...
...AT THE FEVER-PITCH END OF A CONCERT...
..JIMI HENDRIX SETS FIRE TO HIS GUITAR...
HE KNOWS THAT MAGIC ISN'T MADE TO LAST...
ART AT ITS HEIGHT MUST PERISH ...
DESTRUCTION LEADS TO SELF-DESTRUCTION?
HENDRIX DIES IN LONDON IN 1970.. PROBABLY FROM A DRUG OVERDOSE...
THREE WEEKS LATER JANIS JOPLIN DIES IN THE SAME WAY...
BOTH WERE ONLY 27 YEARS OLD! ...

FLY US... MAN!

Van der Plook Free Press incd PRESENTS
ROCK TRIP comix
with many thanks to R. Crumb
JUST AS MAN PREPARES TO PUT HIS BOOT ON THE MOON...
SQUIRT
GLOMP
...IN SAN FRANCISCO
HIGH MAN!
REALLY HIGH!
HAIGHT
ASHBURY
...OTHER ADVENTURERS PREPARE THEMSELVES FOR OTHER ADVENTURES...
HELLOEE? ANYONE HOME!?
...THE HIPPIES THE "FLOWER CHILDREN"...
...WITH THEIR COMMUNES...
...THEIR RITES...
LOVE-IN
...THEIR LACONIC HIP WORD SYSTEMS...
HIP
HIGH MAN
YEAH
TURN ON
FAR OUT
DIG
CRAZY
DROP OUT MAN
I FLIPPED MAN
"THE SACRAMENTS OF MARIJUANA AND L.S.D. MUST ONLY BE TAKEN"...
...UNDER THE INFLUENCE OF HALLUCINAGENIC DRUGS
..."BY INITIATES AND PRIESTS OF THE RELIGION"...
...AND OF GURUS LIKE TIMOTHY LEARY...
..."AND THIS ONLY IN TEMPLES"...
...ARE GOING TO GIVE BIRTH TO A COUNTER-CULTURE...
THE
ROCK culture

..AND TO A NEW SOUND.
THE NEW GROUPS ...
COUNTRY JOE & THE FISH
I'M THE FISH...
..WHERE'S COUNTRY JOE?
GRATEFUL DEAD
JEFFERSON AIRPLANE
"SURREALISTIC PILLOW"..
GRACE SLICK
"WORKING MAN'S DEAD"
JERRY GARCIA
"VINTAGE DEAD"
"LIVE DEAD"
CANNED HEAT
"ON THE ROAD AGAIN"
MOBY GRAPE
electric prunes
STEVE MILLER
Love
FUGS
...USE DRUGS TO PROBE ...
... DELVE ... MELT ...
TO FLEE THE PATHS AND THE CODES...
PSYDHEDELIC ART IS A SOUVENIR OF THE TRIPS OF ACID-ROCK ! ...
THE UNDERGROUND MOVEMENT HAS ITS HEROES ... ...
KLIK
KLIK
KLIK
KLIK
KLIK
FRITZ the CAT
ANOTHER PUSSY!
AND ITS MARTYRS ...
CHEAP THRILLS
... THE MAGNIFICENT BLUESEY JANIS JOPLIN OF BIG BROTHER & THE HOLDING COMPANY...
...AND JIM MORRISON MESSIAH OF THE (WIDE OPENING) DOORS ... ...
NO JIM NO!
...WHO DIES IN HIS BATH IN PARIS IN 1971 ...
...AND SO WE COME TO THE END ...
THE END?
THE END
60'
THE END
...OF THE '60s ...
THE END!

WOODSTOCK - THE FINAL FLING OF THE BROTHERHOOD OF ROCK BEFORE THE SPLINTERED '70s … …
SOME PEACE AND QUIET!
I'M OFF TO THE ISLE OF WIGHT!
GET THAT, MOLES, IT'S JIMI HENDRIX!
I'M JUST NUTS ABOUT JIMI …
… JIVERNATE SQUIRREL!
woodstock
3 DAYS OF PEACE MUSIC & LOVE
JOAN BAEZ. BUTTERFIELD BLUES BAND. CANNED HEAT. JOE COCKER. COUNTRY JOE & THE FISH. CROSBY STILLS NASH & YOUNG. ARLO GUTHRIE. RICHIE HAVENS. JIMI HENDRIX. TEN YEARS AFTER. SANTANA. JOHN B. SEBASTIAN. JEFFERSON AIRPLANE. COUNTRY JOE Mc DONALD. SHA-NA-NA. SLY & THE FAMILY STONE. THE WHO.
JIMI… H… E… N… WHAT?
HENDRIX! PAGE 66
B.D. Rock

THE SEVENTIES
NEW DIRECTIONS

THANKS TO MAKE-UP, GREASE PAINT, PLASTIC SURGERY AND TRANSPLANTS ... ...
...THE FACE OF ROCK CONTINUES TO CHANGE THROUGHOUT THE 70s! ... ...
LEAVE THAT QUIFF ALONE!
MILES DAVIS - THE MATCHMAKER BETWEEN JAZZ AND ROCK ("BITCHES BREW" 1969).
MILES DAVIS
MUSICAL MARRIAGES ARRANGED
ROCK: PLAYFUL, DYNAMIC YOUNG THING SEEKS CREATIVE PARTNER FOR IMPROVISATIONS AND... WHO KNOWS
JAZZ ROCK
HERBIE HANCOCK
CHICAGO
CARLOS SANTANA
I SAID THAT!
BLOOD SWEAT & TEARS
CHURCHILL
WAYNE SHORTER
JOE ZAWINUL
WEATHER REPORT
JOHN McLAUGHLIN
MAHAVISHNU ORCHESTRA
CLASSY!
Return to Forever
CHICK COREA
STANLEY CLARKE
JAZZ: NOW "CULTURED MUSIC" ASSOCIATES WITH A SLIGHTLY LESS STYLISH PARTNER...
IN OTHER KITCHENS... STRANGE BREWS ARE CONCOCTED BY THE INGENIOUS FRANK ZAPPA (AND THE MOTHERS OF INVENTION)
200 Motels
...MIXING JAZZ, SYMPHONIC MUSIC, CONCRETE MUSIC, BIKES ETC... ...
FRANK ZAPPA "DOES THIS SORT OF LIFE LOOK INTERESTING TO YOU?"
SAPRISTI!
ZIS ROCK I DEEG!
PIERRE BOULEZ
...WHO APPEARS IN CONCERT WITH ZAPPA!
SIMPLE, PRIMITIVE ROCK GIVES ITSELF A SHOT OF GREY MATTER ... ...
VERY CLEVER THAT RIFF ARNOLD!...
NOW TH IS BRAIN ROCK!

BUT... IN DECADENT NEW YORK A NEW ROCK GROWS WITH POISON AS ITS SAP... ...
THE FACTORY... THE LOFT-SALON OF THE ARTIST ANDY WARHOL... THE BIG STARS? - VELVET UNDERGROUND...
JOHN CALE
WHO'S HE THINK HE IS? MADAME DE SEVIGNE!
LOU REED
"FEMME FATALE"
NICO
Campbell's TOMATO SOUP
Urban Rock
CITY-SICK TRASH ROCK
NEON-LIT...
SUNKEN EYED GROUPS, DERELICT HEROES HAUNT THE ALLEY-WAYS OF ROCK... ... ...
"TAKE ME TO THE RIVER" 1978
...TALKING HEADS SING OF THE NEW METROPOLITAN MALAISE...
"HEART OF GLASS"
Chelsea
HOTEL
max's Kansas city
...PATTI SMITH, STRANGE, OFF-BEAT GUITARIST-POET...
DAVID JOHANSEN
"BECAUSE THE NIGHT"
"TOO MUCH TOO SOON" 1974
...DEBBIE HARRY... ...(BLONDIE) PERVERSE LITTLE ROCK-LOLITA...
HEY... JULIET, IT'S ROMEO RAYMOND!
...THE NEW YORK DOLLS, THEIR TRANSVESTITE TRIPS AND THEIR CHEAP GLITTER!...
SNIFF
"HEROÏN"
"A WALK ON THE WILD SIDE"
"NOW I WANNA SNIFF SOME GLUE"
...THE RADICAL RAMONES - COLD AND HARD...
...THE AMBIVALENT LOU REED, EX-VELVET UNDERGROUND...
THE FLOWERS OF EVIL OF THE ASPHALT JUNGLE!...

AFTER THE SORDID NEW YORK SCENE A TOUCH OF ENGLISH CLASS ...
IN A WORLD OF HAPPENINGS PINK FLOYD DEVISE ...
ART ROCK
"PIPER AT THE GATES OF DAWN" 1967
"THE DARK SIDE OF THE MOON" 1973
CLIP FROM THE PINK FLOYD FILM "THE WALL" 1982
PINK FLOYD DONATION
HMMM! INTERESTING
GOT THE CATALOGUE?
?
...A MULTI-MEDIA EVENT COMBINING MUSIC, LIGHT SHOW, LASER, QUADROPHONIC SOUND...
DECIDEDLY POST-ARTAUD!
PRECISELY!
...ROCK IS NO LONGER A LINEAR MUSIC ...
SSHH..
DIVINE
...BUT A SONOROUS SHIFTING MASS...
...CREATING IMAGES, WORLDS ...
HOW NOVEL!
I SWOON!
OVER ...
... ... WHELMING

"THE RETURN OF THE GIANT HOGWEED" 1971
"THE FOUNTAIN OF SALMACIS"
PETER GABRIEL
"LARK'S TONGUES IN ASPIC"
...THE COMPOSITIONS OF GENESIS ARE COMPLEX, ELABORATE MUSICALLY INVOLVED
WHOOPS! PASS ME THE SECATEURS
NURSERY CRYME ROOM
...THE FOUNTAIN OF SALMACIS TURNS YOU INTO A HERMAPHRODITE
MIND THE SPLASH!
MY MANHOOD!
THE SOUL OF GENESIS ...
...THE WAY-OUT VISIONS OF KING CRIMSON...
LOOKS GREAT ON THE WALL...
THAT MUSIC...

"FLESH AND BLOOD" 1980
EXHIBITIONIST !
HOW FUTURIST, MY DEAR BRIAN.
HOW DECADENT, MY DEAR BRYAN
EGO-TRIP!
YES
"ASTRAL TRAVELLER"
"TAKING TIGER MOUNTAIN BY STRATEGY"
HEY! WHERE ARE MY SHADES?
...YES - A MUSICAL STATE OF GRACE...
...CHIC, DECADENT, THE SUBTLE COLORS OF ROXY MUSIC ... ...
QUITE SO!
BRYAN FERRY
BRIAN ENO
THE FUTURIST COMPOSITIONS OF BRIAN ENO (EX ROXY MUSIC)
...ALL THESE MAKE UP THE PALETTE OF ART ROCK...
CAN'T UNDERSTAND A WORD
THAT'S HEAD ROCK COOKIE!

... ART ROCK REVEALS THE EXISTENCE OF OTHER WORLDS ...
TRANSCENDENTAL FEET
SPACE ROCK
... PROVIDES A MEANS OF REACHING THEM
... A REPETITIVE COSMIC ROCK ...
COSMIC STRING
... OBSESSIONAL ...
... ONTOLOGICAL ...
... MEDITATIVE ...
... A ROCK USING SYNTHESISERS ...
MADE IN GERMANY BY ...
REALITY BALLAST.
KRAFTWERK
Amon Düül
TANGERINE DREAM
KLAUS SCHULZE
FAUST

... ALONGSIDE THIS COSTLY, COMPLEX, MENACING, WEIRD ROCK ...
... EXISTS A SIMPLE ROCK - A VOICE ... A SONG ...
... AN EVERYDAY ROCK EASY TO GET ALONG WITH. THE ...
BALLAD ROCK
JAMES TAYLOR "YOU'VE GOT A FRIEND" 1971
CARLY SIMON "NO SECRETS"
RANDY NEWMAN "SHORT PEOPLE" 1977
TV GUIDE
BILLY JOEL "JUST THE WAY YOU ARE" 1977
HONESTY
LOVELY!

1973: THE START OF THE RECESSION
YOM KIPPUR WAR
...OH GOD... I JUST MUST GET AWAY FROM IT ALL...
FIRST ROCK FOLLY OF THE '70s TO SEND THE PLANET SPINNING ... ...
MY AUNTY'S HEART-THR...
Glamour Rock
MAE WEST
Liberace
MARC BOLAN
MARC BOLAN (T. REX) MARRIES GLAMOUR AND CHARM
ROD STEWART (EX - FACES) GLAMOUR AND SEX.
ROD STEWART
...SEQUINS AND SATIN, GLOSS AND GLITTER... EXTRAVAGANCE (DARLING...) AT LAST!
...BUT FOR WILD, CRAZY GLAMOUR IT'S
...REGINALD DWIGHT...
...WHO COMPOSES (WITH BERNIE TAUPIN) SOME GREAT HITS...
...AND SOME ULTRA-KITSCH NUMBERS!...
?!?!?!
"YOUR SONG"
... I FEEL SO STUPID!
...YOU LOOK BOOTIFUL...
IF MOTHER COULD SEE ME NOW!
"CANDLE IN THE WIND"
"GOODBYE YELLOW BRICK ROAD"
...GLAMOUR, THE MAGIC WHICH TURNS Mr DWIGHT INTO...
Elton John
ROCK PLAYMATE
TECHNICOLO ELTON EVE SETS THE STEPPES ON FIRE.
ЭLTOИ!
ЭLTOИ!
...OVER THE TOP... OUT OF THIS WORLD...
FROM THE FILM: "TO RUSSIA WITH ELTON"

...WITH David Bowie, GLAMOUR BECOMES AN ART FORM...
...HIS BODY AN EMPTY CANVAS...
...BOWIE, LIKE "THE MAN WHO FELL TO EARTH" (FILM BY NICOLAS ROEG 1976)...
...IS AMBIGUOUS, FASCINATING, REMOTE, AN ARTIST WHOSE APPEARANCE CHANGES WITH THE CLIMATE OF THE MUSIC
1980
Scary Monsters
April 1973
Aladdin Sane
May 73
1974
The Man who sold the World
1971
1979
Just a gigolo
1981
Baal
1972
BOWIE EVEN CREATES HIS OWN ALTER EGO... ZIGGY STARDUST... AN IMAGE OF... HIMSELF!!
IT'S THE WATERGATE SYNDROME... (WHO IS WHO?)...
...SCHIZO ROCK...
BERTOLT BRECHT
...PSSST...RAYMOND ...THEY... ER... DON'T LOOK TERRIBLY MANLY!
THEY'RE ANDROGYNOUS, COOKIE... THE IN-THING...
ANDRO... ANG... WHAT'S THE POINT?...
THEY WANT TO SHOCK, COOKIE... DISTURB... BE DIFFERENT, AND THEN... WHO KNOWS?... GIRLS IDENTIFY WITH THE BOYS WHO LOOK LIKE GIRLS?
NOT ME!!
GOOD THING THERE'S YOU, RAYMOND!...
WELL... ACTUALLY.
ONE MUST KEEP ABREAST OF THE TIMES COOKIE!!

AFTER THE AMBIGUITIES OF GLAMOUR ... A BREATH OF FRESH AIR ... A CLEAN CALIFORNIAN ROCK, "COOL" CLEVER, LAID-BACK BUT ELECTRIC ... ...
FLEETWOOD MAC, OF ENGLISH EXTRACTION MAKE THE BIG TIME IN LOS ANGELES WITH THE BITTER-SWEET ALBUM "RUMOURS" ONE OF THE MEGA-HITS OF THE 70s ... ...
WEST COAST
...THIS IS KSAN YOUR LOCAL ROCK RADIO STATION...
The Doobie Brothers LONG TRAIN RUNNIN'
FLEETWOOD MAC
AND THEN ... FOUR BRILLIANT, CUDDLY CHARACTERS WHO DELIGHT THE WORLD ... ...
EAGLES
...(DAVID) CROSBY...
...(STEPHEN) STILLS...
...(GRAHAM) NASH...
...(NEIL) & YOUNG!...
"LONG TIME GONE" 1969
"SUITE: JUDY BLUE EYES"
"49 BYE BYES"
Hotel California
KTD 251
A "WELL-TEMPERED" ROCK
THIS IS MOOD ROCK ... SHOWERS, SMILES, MISTS AND MELANCHOLY ... ...

ND AFTER THE URBAN "COOL"... A COUNTRY "COOL"...
THE AUTHENTICITY OF RUSTIC ROCK IS COMPROMISED BY THE COMMERCIAL SUCCESS OF ... ...
NASHVILLE
HANK WILLIAMS (DIES IN 1953) 100% PURE-NO ADDITIVES
...AND ITS STARS...
CASHVILLE
JOHNNY CASH "LIVE AT SAN QUENTIN"
TRASHVILLE
WILLIE NELSON
...A COMMERCIAL SUCCESS CONTESTED (AND IMITATED!!!) BY THE NEW STYLE.
COUNTRY ROCK
THE NEW ANCH ROCKERS...
WILLIE NELSON, THE OUTLAW WITH HIS OWN BRAND OF BLUE JEANS...
CHARLIE RICH
"THE MOST BEAUTIFUL GIRL"
DOLLY PARTON
WAYLON JENNINGS
"LADIES LOVE OUTLAWS"
EMMYLOU HARRIS
PARIS TEXAS
STOP THAT MAN!
...AND ON THE WILD FRONTIERS... A SIMPLE AGGRESSIVE BOOGIE ROCK
CREEDENCE CLEARWATER REVIVAL
"GREEN RIVER"
"PROUD MARY" 1969
...AND IN THE SWAMP LANDS OF THE SOUTH, A ROCK THAT'S RAUNCHY, TOUGH... BUT ACCIDENT-PRONE
JACK DANIEL'S
...THE VOICE OF JOHN FOGERTY EVOKES THE SMELL OF CUT GRASS AND HICKORY WOOD...
ANDRE... THE ROWING POET...
"SWAMP MUSIC"
LYNYRD SKYNYRD -WIPED OUT IN A PLANE CRASH IN 1977...
...THE ALLMAN BROTHERS... BY TWO FREAK IDENTICAL MOTORCYCLE ACCIDENTS IN 1971 AND 1972...
"WHIPPING POST"
WATCH OUT CATS!
THE NEXT PAGE! WOW!
WANT SOME COTTON WOOL
I'VE GOT MY EAR PLUGS...
KLU
KLUK
GLUG

IN THE MID '50s ROCK WAS BAD-MANNERED, UNSOCIABLE ... NOW "COUNTRIFIED", "GLAMOURIZED", TUNEFUL AND TAMED ... IS ROCK LOSING ITS IDENTITY ? ... ...
hard rock
LED ZEPPELIN
... AND HEAVY METAL (SON OF HARD) REVER TO THE TOUGH (GRRRR RAW STYLE OF PRIMITIVE ROCK ... ...
?
THE EARTH SHAKES, THE SKY IS DARKENED... BY THE FLIGHT OF THE VALKYRIES OF ROCK, THE GODS OF HEAVY METAL.
WAGNER IS A LULLABY BY COMPARISON...
"A NIGHT AT THE OPERA"
FREDDY MERCURY (QUEEN)
VAN HALEN
TED NUGENT
RITCHIE BLACKMORE (DEEP PURPLE)
PHIL LYNOTT (THIN LIZZY)
PHIL TAYLOR (MOTÖRHEAD)
ROBERT PLANT (LED ZEPPELIN)
ERIC BLOOM (BLUE ÖYSTER CULT)
THE TRADE MARK OF HEAVY METAL - VICIOUS EXTRAVAGANCE !!
IT'S SADO_MACHO (!) ROCK ! ...
... LEATHER, MUSCLES, TATTOOS, NAZISM AND NAILS, ALL THE TRAPPINGS OF A TEUTONIC GLADIATOR...

...THE NEW RULERS OF ROCK PREPARE FOR ARMAGEDDON ... ...
Queen
Judas Priest
Deep Purple
Iron Maiden
Led Zep
Scorpions
Mötorhead
Blue Oyster Cult
Rose Tattoo
Saxon
Status Quo
...THEIR WEAPONS? GUITAR RIFFS SHOT FROM THE HIP... AND A VOLUME THAT KILLS... ...
DAZED AND C
*"DAZED AND CONFUSED" (LED ZEPPELIN)
8 POINTS ON THE RICHTER SCALE...
... AND BLACK MAGIC!! - HARD ROCK IS OFTEN SUSPECTED OF HAVING SATANIC TENDENCIES...
BLACK SABBATH AND "SATAN ROCK"
ALICE COOPER, WHO PREACHES NECROPHILIA ...
NO, I AM NOT A RAVEN!
KISS
KINGS IN SATAN'S SERVICE
AC/DC
ALTERNATING CURRENT OR ANTI CHRIST & DEATH TO CHRIST
LED ZEPPELIN IN "STAIRWAY TO HEAVEN"
ROCK SHOCKS... ROCK IS EVIL!...
... BUT TO EVERY STORY A MORAL, TO EVERY GOD A TWILIGHT... ...
THE SEARCH FOR SHOCK LEADS TO EXCESS AND EXCESS TO DECADENCE ... ...
... WAY-OUT GEAR, MAKE UP, TONS OF EQUIPMENT, LASERS, LIGHTS, LOOT ... ...
THEY'RE OUT OF THEIR MINDS
JOHNNY ROTTEN
BETWEEN PERFORMER AND SPECTATOR THE ABYSS WIDENS AND ROCK LOOKS LIKE IT'S FALLING INTO IT...

ULTIMATELY HARD ROCK ALIENATES ... YOU PAY YOUR MONEY AND YOU ADMIRE THE GODS FROM AFAR ...
VILLAGE PEOPLE "MACHO MAN"
DONNA SUMMER
...BUT THANKS TO DISCO, YOU TOO CAN BECOME A GOD. ALL YOU HAVE TO DO IS GET UP AND DANCE
ABBA "DANCING QUEEN" 1977
DISCO
THE BEE GEES "JIVE TALKING" 1975 "HOW DEEP IS YOUR LOVE" 1977
...SO, AT THE WEEKEND, UNDER THE CRYSTAL BALL OF THE DISCOTHEQUE ... MR AVERAGE ... ...
?!
TURNS INTO PRINCE CHARMING
...(SEE MY ARTICLE "ROCK AND THE CINDERELLA SYNDROME")
THE SATURDAY NIGHT CHOICE? SIMPLE! ...
TO BEE GEE OR NOT TO BEE GEE !!
SATURDAY NIGHT FEVER 1978
JOHN TRAVOLTA
DISCO MAKES MONEY FOR EVERYONE - EVEN FOR THE BUILDING INDUSTRY...
...IN '78, 36 MILLIONS AMERICANS TAKE TO THE FLOOR IN 20,000 DISCOS! ... ...
...AND THE MUSIC? HIGH PITCHED SENSUAL VOICES SET AGAINST AN INSISTENT HEAVY BEAT
...AND WHEN DISCO FLAGS, FUNK IS WAITING IN THE WINGS.

... DAZED AND DIZZY AFTER THE DISCO DELIGHTS...
DISCO

... YOU SINK INTO A COMFY CHAIR...

... TO TAKE IN A CONCERT...

... OF POST MOODY BLUES FIREWORKS MUSIC ... IT'S ...

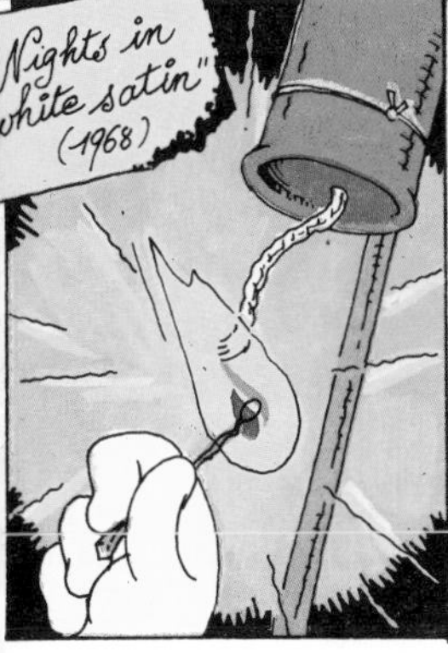

SYMPHO ROCK

WITH THEIR INVENTIVE MELODIC LINE, THEIR ELEGANT TIMBRES ...

Supertramp

WOO THE WORLD!

"CRIME OF THE CENTURY"

"BREAKFAST IN AMERICA" (1979)

THE MULTI-INSTRUMENTALIST PETER FRAMPTON

"SHOW ME THE WAY" (1976)

BOSTON

...AND THE MULTI-TRACK MAGICIAN TOM SCHOLZ

"MORE THAN A FEELING" (1976)

...THE ETHEREAL GUITARS, THE GRAND KEYBOARD CADENZAS OF

KANSAS

"DUST IN THE WIND" (1978)

STYX

WITH ITS CLASSICAL OVER/UNDERTONES (!)

"BABE" (1979)

"COME SAIL AWAY" (1978)

...ARPEGGIOS, CRESCENDOS, COUNTER-POINT, TUTTI ...

... IF ONLY LUDWIG COULD HEAR ME ...

SYMPHO ROCK IS VERY ECLECTIC - DISCO VOCALS, HARD ROCK RIFFS, ART ROCK POMP, COOKED IN A RICH STUDIO SAUCE ...

...AND SERVED UP IN STADIUMS BEFORE THE HUNGRY MULTITUDES.

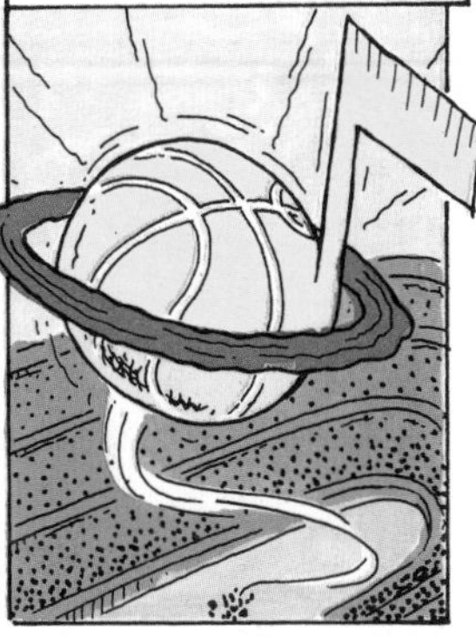

...SYMPHO ROCK MAKES A WHOLE LOT OF MONEY...

...AS THE ROCK AUDIENCE EXPANDS...

SWEAT GIVES WAY TO CHANEL!

BUT... THEN CAME PUNK... VIOLENT, DESTRUCTIVE, ANTI-GLAMOUR, ANTI-CHIC, GOBBING VENOM, SPITTING BILE...
KILLER!
PUNK
NO FUTURE
GET A SNIFF OF THAT!!
WHAT FUN!
THEY'RE DANCING THE POGO!...
YOUNG PEOPLE HAVING A GOOD TIME!
HOW SUPER!
IN MARCH '77 (THE QUEEN'S JUBILEE YEAR) A & M RECORDS SIGNS A CONTRACT WITH THE SEX PISTOLS OUTSIDE BUCKINGHAM PALACE! ...
GREAT GLU MAN!!!
THE HAVES AND THE HAVE-NOTS RUB SHOULDERS ...
LET'S SEE THE LOOT CITY SLICKER!!
SEX PISTOLS
ANARCHY IN THE U.K.
DESTROY
BROMLEY CONTINGENT
NOWHERE
PUNK (A WORD FIRST USED BY ZAPPA? TOWNSHEND? SHAKESPEARE?) IS THE BRAINCHILD OF ...
...MALCOLM McLAREN (AUTHOR OF "THE GREAT ROCK'N'ROLL SWINDLE")... THE GURU BEHIND...
...JOHNNY ROTTEN AND THE SEX-PISTOLS
NOW THAT BOY'S GOT A FUTURE..
BEAUTY? BOURGEOIS BULLSHIT!
TALENT? SCREW TALENT!
JUST DO YER THING WITH WHAT YOU GOT...
BURRP!
GUITAR SOLOS? UP MY NOSE!
WRAP YER EAR AROUND.
NEVER MIND THE BOLLOCKS HERE'S THE SEX PISTOLS
BEER

THE ULTIMATE PUNK SYMBOL? THE SAFETY PIN ... ...
...WITH ITS CONNOTATIONS OF NAPPIES* AND MUTILATION ... THE CHEAP AND NASTY PIN HOLDS TOGETHER THE BITS AND PIECES OF DUSTBIN FASHION...
BRAINTRASH! PUKE FACE!
AT THE ROOTS OF PUNK ... ... UNEMPLOYMENT, BOREDOM, DESPAIR, POVERTY
JOB CENTRE
MAKES YOU FEEL AMBITIOUS!
WANTED: STAFF FOR JOB CENTRES
DEATH OF SID VICIOUS
ULLUUURRRP
AND ... IN THE CASE OF THE PISTOL'S DRUMMER, TRAGIC NIHILISM ...
I'M STUCK ON THIS BOOK!
OVERDOSE
GUTTER PRESS!
PUNK EXPLODES - THE SLITS, THE DAMNED, SIOUXIE AND THE BANSHEES, THE STRANGLERS, THE CLASH
IAN DURY
...THE JAM ... DESCENDENTS OF THE WHO...
SANDINISTA
... AND THE PUNK ANTHEM 'SEX AND DRUGS AND ROCK'N' ROLL"
PAUL WELLER (JAM)
AND ALWAYS THAT GAPING LEERING MOUTH WITH ITS INFLAMED TONSILS AND CHEAP FILLINGS...
JOE STRUMMER (CLASH)
NINA HAGEN
...WITH HER MASTURBATION CLASSES ON GERMAN T.V. ...

* DIAPERS -

A SECOND SHOT IN THE ARM FOR ROCK... A JAMAICAN AFRO-SOUL BORN OUT OF SKA, ROCKSTEADY, BLUE BEAT...

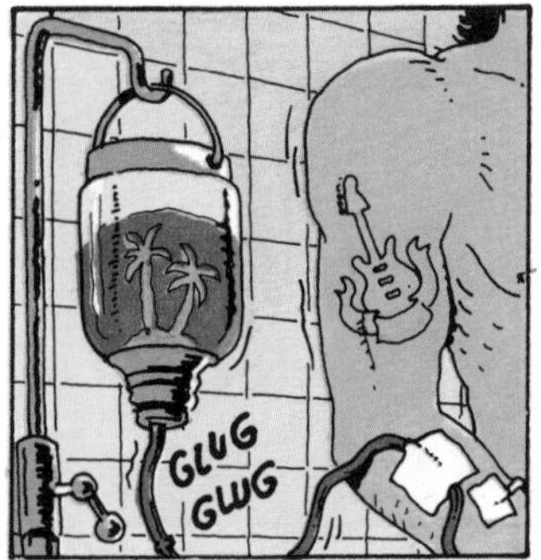

...WHICH FROM KINGSTON TO THE LONDON GHETTOS SINGS WHAT IT MEANS TO BE DEPRIVED...*

BOB MARLEY - THE RASTAFARIAN "GANJA" SMOKING SON OF A WHITE ENGLISH ARMY CAPTAIN, IS - WITH HIS WOOL CAP AND DREADLOCKS - THE PROPHET OF...
Reggae
...HIS CHANTING MUSIC SINGS THE BLUES ("NO WOMAN NO CRY") AND RESISTANCE.

THE "BLACK JAGGER" DIES IN 1981, HIS RED GIBSON BURIED BESIDE HIM...

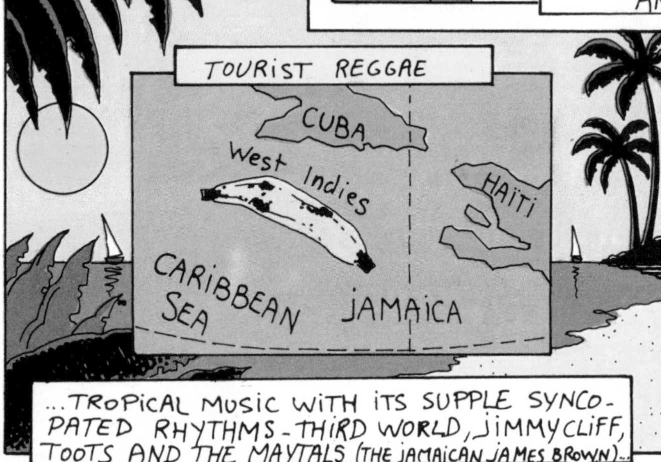

...TROPICAL MUSIC WITH ITS SUPPLE SYNCOPATED RHYTHMS - THIRD WORLD, JIMMY CLIFF, TOOTS AND THE MAYTALS (THE JAMAICAN JAMES BROWN)...

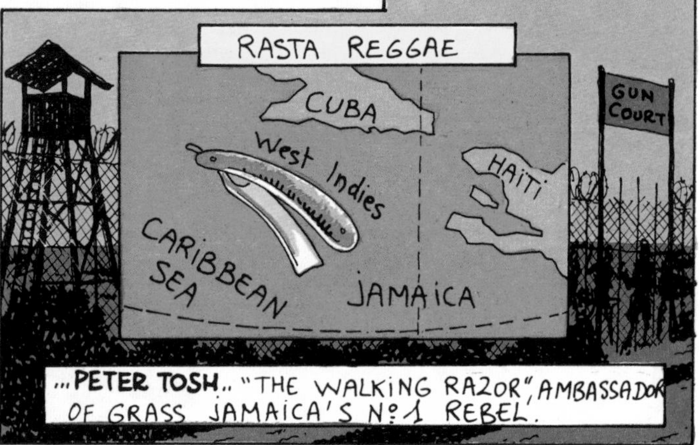

...PETER TOSH.. "THE WALKING RAZOR", AMBASSADOR OF GRASS JAMAICA'S No 1 REBEL.

PETER TOSH!

YOU CAN KEEP THE DOLLARS... GIVE BACK THE EMERALDS, THE RUBIES, THE DIAMONDS ...LET THE PROPHECY COME TRUE...

LEGALIZE IT

BEHIND REGGAE THE RASTAFARIAN RELIGION... THE LOST TRIBE ADRIFT IN THE WHITE MAN'S BABYLON WILL EVENTUALLY RETURN TO ETHIOPIA WHERE THE NEGUS ONCE RULED, THE BLACK EMPEROR OF THE PROMISED LAND.

?

* POST "SKA-IST" BRITISH STYLE, MADNESS AND THE SPECIALS WITH THEIR "RUDE BOY" LOOK, ROCK A NEW STYLE DEPRIVATION... UNEMPLOYMENT!

OVER THE FROZEN WASTES OF ROCK AT THE END OF THE '70S _ SWEPT BY THE BITTER NORTH WIND OF PUNK AND THE WARM SOUTH WIND OF REGGAE THERE DAWNS.
NEW WAVE
THIS ROCK IS STRAIGHT FORWARD
...NO NEED TO BE AS PRO AS CLAPTON
AS RICH AS ELTON.
AS BEAUTIFUL AS BOWIE.
...ON MY RIGHT? THE "COOL" NEW WAVE - CLEAN AND COLD ... ...
...ON MY LEFT, THE NEW WAVE THAT MELTS THE ICE ...
...THE B 52 ...
KINGS OF THE BOPPER'S HOP! ...
... ICY ... ORCHESTRAL MANOEUVRES IN THE DARK ... ...
AND THE GENIUS OF NEW WAVE: ELVIS (SIGH) COSTELLO (...BUDDY HOLLY REINCARNATED?)
...EVEN LOBOTOMIZED (!) DEVO... AUTOMATON ROCK..
CAN'T HEAR A THING!
... '77 - '85 ... 10 ALBUMS ... WITH LYRICS THAT ARE BITTER, IRONIC POLITICAL, TENDER ... ALL DELIVERED IN A CLEAR POST-'60s STYLE ... ...
"JOCKO-HOMO MONGOLOÏD"
'78 - '79 ... THE EXPLOSION RE-EXPLODES...
...WE ARE ENTERING THE AGE OF COMPLEX FASHION...
NEW WAVE ENGENDERS NEW MUSIC...
... WHICH BLOWS HOT ... ...
THE POLICE WITH ECHOES OF JAZZ AND REGGAE ...
POLICE
ROXANNE
MESSAGE IN A BOTTLE
NEW YORK
POLICE
...JOE JACKSON, HIS IRONY, HIS ANGER ... "LOOK SHARP" (1979)
XTC HALF-PUNK HALF-ART
SENSES WORKING OVERTIME
BLACK SEA
WHITE MUSIC
MAKING PLANS FOR NIGEL
...WHICH BLOWS COLD...
...HUMAN LEAGUE AND THE "COLD-WAVE"... AN ANGUISHED TORMENTED MUSIC WITH SYNTHESIZER ICING ...
...AND JOY DIVISION (THE RED LIGHT DISTRICT IN CONCENTRATION CAMPS) ROMANTIC ... GRAVE... DAMNED ...
THE FUN'S FOR TOMORROW ...
JUST A MOMENT, CATS

AND NOW... THE REFLECTIONS OF AN ERA!...
MAGICAL MYSTERY DOOR
... LOVE ...
"TWO VIRGINS" (1968)
"DOUBLE FANTASY" (1980)
... PROTEST ...
"POWER TO THE PEOPLE"
... CREATIVITY...
"SCARED"
... ANGUISH...
... DIVORCE ...
... BETRAYAL (?) ...
"HOW DO YOU SLEEP AT NIGHT"
... RETREAT ... SILENCE ...
...AND THEN...
JL
DECEMBER 8TH 1980, THE DAKOTA 72ND AND CENTRAL PARK WEST ... ...
IMAGINE...
...THE LEGEND...
STATUE OF JOHN LENNON, STRAWBERRY FIELDS, CENTRAL PARK N.Y.C.

THE EIGHTIES

TRENDS AND BENDS

AND WHO iS Mr FUNK ?
(HARD BLACK DISCO)
JOHN TRAVOLTA

WHO DANCES LIKE A GOD ?..

WHO LiVES ALONE WITH HIS VERY SPECiAL PETS ?...
MY HOME

WHO iS NICE AND CLEAN ?!?

WHO iS CHASTE ?

WHO iS THE PiNOCCHiO OF POP ?
QUINCY JONES

MiCHAEL SWELLS THE JACKSON MiLLiONS (BY '83 THE FAMiLY HAD ALREADY SOLD 100 MiLLiON RECORDS. A RECORD MOUNTAiN SOME 252 MiLES HiGH!) ...

THRILLER
MICHAEL JACKSON $120 000 000 FOR "THRILLER"
TV GUIDE
NEWS
MICHAEL JACKSON
... AFTER "OFF THE WALL" ('79)... THE WORLD SHATTERING SUCCESS OF "THRILLER" ('82) THE ViDEO IS BY JOHN LANDiS...

SUCCESS OF SUCH A MAGNiTUDE (HUBRiS ?) THAT MiCHAEL SUFFERS FROM
...OVERKILL OR PUBLiC...
iNDi...
PARDON
...GESTION
BURRRP

SYMBOL OF THIS NEW-FOUND ALL-AMERICAN VITALITY...(AFTER THE TRAUMA OF VIETNAM...) A GENTLEMAN FROM THE WEST...
SPORTSWEAR JANE FONDA
... ONE KING RONALD ...
THE "MIAMI SOUND" OF K.C. AND THE SUNSHINE BAND SWINGS BACK INTO FASHION..
FROM NOW ON, YOU'RE NOT NAIVE IF YOU HAVE A GOOD TIME ... ...
... YOU'RE NOT STUPID IF YOU SMILE, NOT CRASS WHEN YOU SING LOVE SONGS ... ...
THE COMMODORES WITH LIONEL RITCHIE "ENDLESS LOVE"
...THIS NEW POSITIVE ROCK ENERGY BECOMES A PHILOSOPHY ... ...
EARTH
"WHAT WE ARE TRYING TO GET ACROSS WITH OUR MUSIC IS OPTIMISM ..." MAURICE WHITE
THE BRASSY SOUND OF E.W.& F. MELTS THE ICE OF THE NEW WAVE SYNTHESIZERS ...
WIND
& FIRE
"BOOGIE WONDERLAND" 79
"RAISE" 81
"POWERLIGHT" 83
...AND A SPORT !
GRACE JONES
... PHYSICAL (!)...
... HEALTHY(?) ROCK ...
ATHLETIC (WOW)
... ACROBATIC (OUCH!)
...DISCIPLINED (AAA!)
... THE BREAKDANCE
...AND THE SMURF !
STREET DANCE
STREET DANCE
STREET DANCE

AFTER OPULENT FUNK... ... BASIC ROCK!
THE WORKING CLASS ENERGY OF Mr SPRINGSTEEN THE DEEP THROAT OF NEW JERSEY!...
SPRINGSTEEN THE ROCKER WHO REALLY WORKS FOR HIS MONEY!
LANK HAIR SHAGGY SIDEBURNS = TO HELL WITH THE CHIC!
I WAS BORN IN THE U.S.A.
TEE-SHIRT = YOUNG NON-BOURGEOIS AND PROUD OF IT..
BRUCE SPRINGSTEEN
ROCK'S MOST FAMOUS ARM-PIT...
EASY-GOING DO IT YOURSELF ELECTRICS...
WEDDING RING = RESPECT FOR SOCIAL CONVENTIONS
THE GUITAR? A FENDER TELECASTER JUST LIKE IN THE GOOD OLD DAYS..
WITH THE BACKING OF THE E STREET BAND (AND NO DRUGS) SPRINGSTEEN THE PERFECTIONIST HAS FOR THE LAST 15 YEARS SUNG THE MIDDLE "AMERICAN WAY OF LIFE"..
WORN (NON-YUPPY) JEANS
PAY SLIP
NAME:
DATE:
HOURS:
I.D. CARD
V.V.A. VIETNAM VETERANS OF AMERICA
Hungry heart
Wreck on the highway
Clarence Clemons
my brother
Had a brother at the Khe-Shan fighting off the Viet-Cong they still there... He's all gone...
BORN TO RUN
my father's garage
CADILLAC RANCH
GREETINGS FROM ASBURY PARK N.J.
A POETIC REALIST, SPRINGSTEEN IS THE JOHN WAYNE(?) OF ROCK.

..AFTER THE BOUNCING BEAT OF MICHAEL J... ...AFTER THE EMOTIONAL THRUST OF Mr S... THE SEXUAL OOMPH OF PRINCE - THE MARQUIS DE SADO-FUNK!
- PRINCE "A" SIDE - PROVOCATIVE, PORNFUL... SINGING THE UNSPEAKABLE WITH THE VOICE OF AN ANGEL... "SOFT AND WET"... "DIRTY MIND" (THE SEX-ALBUM (?) OF THE DECADE)...
- PRINCE "B" SIDE - THE ROMANTIC ARISTOCRAT - THE "PURPLE RAIN" PERIOD...
OUT OF THE TURBULENT CURRENTS OF THE 80s ... ...AN ISLAND (OF CALM?) PEOPLED BY INVENTIVE, PERSONAL ROCKERS... TOM WAITS... RICKIE LEE JONES... THE CARS...
"ABACAB"
THE DREAMING (82)
...KATE BUSH... CHIC SORCERESS IMMERSED IN GURDJIEFF...
... PHIL COLLINS ... THE GROUCHO MARX OF POST-NEW WAVE PERCUSSION...
ADONNA ("LIKE A VIRGIN" 85) - ALL TULLE AND TILLATION, FLAUNTS E SAME ELECTRIC MIX PRINCE, COMBINING X AND INNOCENCE TO AKE FOR "DIRTY DISCO."
DESPERATELY SEEKING MODESTY!
SEX-SHOP
RESULT? WELL-MEANING AMERICANS FORM GROUPS TO PROTECT YOUTH AGAINST THE RAVAGES OF ROCK......
LYRICS ARE CENSORED, RECORDS BANNED, WE'RE BACK ONCE AGAIN IN 1955
BOY TOY
WHAT A NAUGHTY GIRL!...
... IN EUROPE, ENERGY IS TURNED INTO ENTHUSIASM (A MORE SOPHISTICATED MANIFESTATION OF VITALITY...)
... AND FUN IS BORN.

LOOK
... NOVELTY IS THE GOAL OF THE NEW POST-PUNK, POST-NEW WAVE GENERATION AND THE LOOK IS AS IMPORTANT AS THE MUSIC! ...
THE PIRATE-HUSSAR LOOK
BRAINCHILD OF MALCOLM McLAREN
BRAVO TREMENDOUS
MAGGIE LOOK
Adam and the Ants
THE CHIC-RETRO LOOK.
Style Council
Martin Fry & the group ABC
THE CHIC-COLONIAL LOOK.
PROUD OF YOU!
Heaven 17
THE JET SET CHIC.
THE NEW ROMANTIC
THE TROPICAL FUN LOOK
VOGUE
THE GLOSSY MAG CHIC
NICE LEGS!
PASSPORTS PLEASE!...
Wham!
Sade
(a)
(b)
Duran Duran
Kid Creole & the Coconuts

PARADE
THE MILITANT GAY LOOK
Bronski beat
THE LYRICAL GAY LOOK
Klaus Nomi
THE CLEAN CUT 60s LOOK
Mari Wilson
KEEP IT UP BOYS!
THE FUN GAY LOOK
Frankie goes to Hollywood
"SWEET DREAMS"
Eu ryth mics
THE HARD COUNTRY LOOK
ZZ Top
THE ROCKABILLY REVISITED LOOK
CRAZY RHYTHM!
The Stray Cats
Boy George
GREAT SCOTT!!
AND WHAT ABOUT THE MUSIC?!..
AS ECLECTIC AS THE CLOTHES!... REGGAE, NEW WAVE, DISCO, JAZZ, FUNK...
A BIT OF EVERYTHING... EXOTIC, ECCENTRIC, STUPID, RETRO, KITSCH...
COULD IT BE THAT ROCK IS BECOMING REFERENTIALLY SELF-CONSCIOUS?...
CAN'T UNDERSTAND A WORD HE SAYS...
AND WHAT IF ROCK WAS TO MOVE LEFT? AND WHAT IF "RED WEDGE" WAS THE FUTURE...
BILLY BRAGG AND THE IDEOLOGICAL LOOK.
GASP!
RED WEDGE

BUT... EVEN IN THE LABYRINTHINE WORLD OF THE "LOOK" ROCK REMAINS INTACT ... ...
... LYRICAL IN THE DUBLIN ROCK OF ...
U2
JIM KERR
STARK IN THE GLASGOW ROCK OF SIMPLE MINDS...
... WITHOUT MAKE-UP FUSS OR FINERY... ROCK... NOW AND FOREVER MORE ... A RHYTHM ... A CRY...
STING (POLICE)
... A BASS ...
... A GUITAR ...
MARK KNOPFLE (DIRE STRAITS
ROCK
... ROCK ... PARADISE OR JUNGLE, GOLDMINE OR SLUM, WAY IN OR WAY OUT, PAIN OR BALM ... ..
LYRICISM AT LAST...
... ROCK ... EXULTANT, MEAN, RICH, LEAN, BAROQUE, ACID, BLU ... PLEDGE OF THE NEW LACONIC PARSIFAL ...
... ROCK ... THE GRAIL OF A GENERATION...

Mr RAYMOND CLAIRVOYANT
DRRIIIIING!

...AND EXACTLY WHERE...
...IS ROCK GOING?

I SEE 3 POSSIBLE FUTURES FOR ROCK...
BOURBON WHISKEY

FIRST... TECHNOLOGICAL ADVANCE!

AFTER THE SOUNDIES (OF THE 40s)
...AND THE SCOPI-TONES (OF THE 60s)
THE VIDEO CLIP...
...WHERE ROCK EXPLOITS TO THE FULL THE WHOLE RANGE OF VIDEO TRICKERY...

THIS WAY FOR "ANDRE IN VIDEOLAND

FREEZE FRAME......

WOOOF
FAST FORWARD

DISTORTED PERSPECTIVE...

...NOITCA...

PRULS
...ESREVER...

PSSCHHH
...A WORLD WHERE THE ELEMENTS PREVAIL...

...WHERE FANTASIES ARE FREED... FREAK GIANTS...

...FREAK DWARFS...

A FETISHIST'S DREAM-WORLD (LIBIDO-VIDEO?)

END OF THE JOURNEY TO VIDEOLAND.
...AND THE LONGEST VIDEO IN THE HISTORY OF ROCK?
CLIP JOINT

...THE WORLD-WIDE LIVE-AID CONCERT FOR FAMINE RELIEF IN ETHIOPIA (JULY 13TH 1985: A BILLION AND A HALF T.V. VIEWERS FOR 16-HOURS OF NON-STOP ROCK)

... NEXT... DEIFICATION !!!
... BUT NOT FOR EVERYONE !... ...
... OBLIVION FOR SOME ...
LULU...
... HOUSEWIFE ...
SONNY...
THAT MUST BE ROCKFISH ...
RESTAURANT OWNER
PETE BEST...
BAKER
AS ANDY WARHOL SAYS
... IN THE FUTURE EVERYONE WILL BE A CELEBRITY...
... FOR 15 MINUTES
... ETERNAL GLORY FOR OTHERS ...
FOR... EVEN IN 50 YEARS ... THEY WILL STILL BE WITH US ... ...
MICK JAGGER
HEY !! "SWEET LITTLE SIXTEEN"
JERRY LEE LEWIS
CHUCK BERRY
FATS DOMINO
STEVIE WONDER
DAVID BOWIE
PAUL McCARTNEY
"DO YA THINK I'M SEXY?"
LOU REED
TINA TURNER
ROD STEWART
ELTON JOHN
BOB DYLAN
... THE SUPERMEN... THE GODS OF ROCK ...

... AND FINALLY ...
APOCALYPSE!
ROCK ... ...
... FUTURE MUSIC ...
...OF THE SPHERES ?...
?
PARIS GUIDE
SNAP SNAP
TAP TAP
BILL HALEY!
ONE-O-CLOCK
TWO-O-CLOCK
THREE-O-CLOCK
ROCK!!!!
SLURP MIAM
GREASE
ROCKINDEX ?!
HOW HIC NISHE! Mr. VAN DER HIC... PLOOK.
... BUT OF COURSE Mr. HIC DER ... I MEAN..
GOOD HEAVENS ... WHY WORRY? WE'VE JUST FINISHED ...
CELEBRATING? US?... A NOISE?
... OH ... THAT MUST BE ...
HMM
... THE COMPUTER WARMING UP

I TOLD YOU!...
WE'RE NOT IN IT!!!
GRRRRRRR
REVENGE!!

ROCK T.V.
FAME!
OUR BOOK FEATURED ON T.V.!
HUH... THE MEDIA TRYING TO GET IN ON THE ACT... TYPICAL!
$
AT LAST...
PFF

MY KNEES ... I'M DEAD SCARED...
XXIII ROCK STUDIO
... MUSTN'T OVERDO IT... MUSTN'T PUT THE OTHERS IN THE SHADE..
A GRAVY STAIN OH GOD!

RECORDING
?!
WE'RE LATE !?
THEY CAN'T START WITHOUT US !?
SSSSSHHHH !!
BBBBBBUT ??!!!

NOW MR VAN DER PLOOK YOU ARE THE AUTHOR OF THIS FASCINATING HISTORY OF ROCK...
...THAT IS SO, YES...
...TELL US HOW YOUR BOOK WAS BORN.

LITERARY CREATION IS OBVIOUSLY AT ONCE BOTH EXHILARATING AND EXACTING... IN FACT I'D GO AS FAR AS TO SAY.

VAN DER PLOOK!!

HE'S NOT THE AUTHOR!
FRAUD !!!

WE ARE !!!
THIEF !!!
ITS NOT POSSIBLE
AFTER ALL OUR WORK... BUT ?...

WHAT ???

... IS ...
...HAPPENING

YOU SEE THE VERY NOTION OF ATTRIBUTING IMAGE TO SOUND IS...
?
BAOOOM

MIKE OLDFIELD
SOFT MACHINE
JETHRO TULL
NICE
GARY NUMAN
TODD
MELANIE
WHY LEAVE US OUT ? WE DEMAND A PLACE IN HISTORY !
AAAAAOOOO
CHET ATKINS
CAROLE KING
LOUIS JORDAN
JONI MITCHELL
JOHNNY KIDD
BILL DOGGET
IGGY POP
JORGE BEN
LES PAUL
PHIL OCHS
RUFUS
ROY ORBISON
TAKE THAT!!!
COME COME LADS.
...DON'T TAKE IT SO...
CAT STEVENS
DUANE EDDY

A FEW HOURS LATER... AT THE HOSPITAL.
THAT'S ROCK...
...MR VAN DER PLOOK ...
VIOLENT...
...AGGRESSIVE
...PRIMITIVE
YOU SHOULD READ THIS BOOK...
IT'LL HELP YOU UNDERSTAND...
... CIAO, MR VAN DER PLOOK...
GGHUMFFGRMUMF!

SEE YOU LATER
ALLIGATOR
DOO WOP
DOO WOP
DUTFOY 85